POEMS OF
ELLA WHEELER WILCOX

Ella Wheeler Wilcox

POEMS OF
ELLA WHEELER WILCOX

Poems of Power and
Poems of Passion

BIBLIOBAZAAR

ISBN: 978-1-4346-4714-6

Poems of
Ella Wheeler Wilcox

CONTENTS

POEMS OF POWER

POEMS OF PASSION

POEMS OF POWER

NOTE

The final word in the title of this volume refers to the DIVINE POWER in every human being, the recognition of which is the secret to all success and happiness. It is this idea which many of the verses endeavour to illustrate.

E. W. W.

THE QUEEN'S LAST RIDE

(Written on the day of Queen Victoria's funeral)

The Queen is taking a drive today,
They have hung with purple the carriage-way,
They have dressed with purple the royal track
Where the Queen goes forth and never comes back.

Let no man labour as she goes by
On her last appearance to mortal eye:
With heads uncovered let all men wait
For the Queen to pass, in her regal state.

Army and Navy shall lead the way
For that wonderful coach of the Queen's today.
Kings and Princes and Lords of the land
Shall ride behind her, a humble band;
And over the city and over the world
Shall the Flags of all Nations be half-mast-furled,
For the silent lady of royal birth
Who is riding away from the Courts of earth,
Riding away from the world's unrest
To a mystical goal, on a secret quest.

Though in royal splendour she drives through town,
Her robes are simple, she wears no crown:
And yet she wears one, for, widowed no more,
She is crowned with the love that has gone before,
And crowned with the love she has left behind
In the hidden depths of each mourner's mind.

Bow low your heads—lift your hearts on high—
The Queen in silence is driving by!

THE MEETING OF THE CENTURIES

A curious vision on mine eyes unfurled
    In the deep night. I saw, or seemed to see,
    Two Centuries meet, and sit down vis-à-vis
Across the great round table of the world:
One with suggested sorrows in his mien,
    And on his brow the furrowed lines of thought;
    And one whose glad expectant presence brought
A glow and radiance from the realms unseen.

Hand clasped with hand, in silence for a space
    The Centuries sat; the sad old eyes of one
    (As grave paternal eyes regard a son)
Gazing upon that other eager face.
And then a voice, as cadenceless and gray
    As the sea's monody in winter time,
    Mingled with tones melodious, as the chime
Of bird choirs, singing in the dawns of May.

THE OLD CENTURY SPEAKS

By you, Hope stands. With me, Experience walks.
Like a fair jewel in a faded box,
In my tear-rusted heart, sweet Pity lies.
For all the dreams that look forth from your eyes,
And those bright-hued ambitions, which I know

Must fall like leaves and perish, in Time's snow,
(Even as my soul's garden stands bereft,)
I give you pity! 'tis the one gift left.

THE NEW CENTURY

Nay, nay, good friend! not pity, but Godspeed,
Here in the morning of my life I need.
Counsel, and not condolence; smiles, not tears,
To guide me through the channels of the years.
Oh, I am blinded by the blaze of light
That shines upon me from the Infinite.
Blurred is my vision by the close approach
To unseen shores, whereon the times encroach.

THE OLD CENTURY

Illusion, all illusion. List and hear
The Godless cannons, booming far and near.
Flaunting the flag of Unbelief, with Greed
For pilot, lo! the pirate age in speed
Bears on to ruin. War's most hideous crimes
Besmirch the record of these modern times.
Degenerate is the world I leave to you,—
My happiest speech to earth will be—adieu.

THE NEW CENTURY

You speak as one too weary to be just.
I hear the guns—I see the greed and lust.
The death throes of a giant evil fill
The air with riot and confusion. Ill

Ofttimes makes fallow ground for Good; and Wrong
Builds Right's foundation, when it grows too strong.
Pregnant with promise is the hour, and grand
The trust you leave in my all-willing hand.

THE OLD CENTURY

As one who throws a flickering taper's ray
To light departing feet, my shadowed way
You brighten with your faith. Faith makes the man
Alas, that my poor foolish age outran
Its early trust in God! The death of art
And progress follows, when the world's hard heart
Casts out religion. 'Tis the human brain
Men worship now, and heaven, to them, means—gain.

THE NEW CENTURY

Faith is not dead, tho' priest and creed may pass,
For thought has leavened the whole unthinking mass,
And man looks now to find the God within.
We shall talk more of love, and less of sin,
In this new era. We are drawing near
Unatlassed boundaries of a larger sphere.
With awe, I wait, till Science leads us on,
Into the full effulgence of its dawn.

DEATH HAS CROWNED HIM A MARTYR

(Written on the day of
President McKinley's death)

In the midst of sunny waters, lo! the mighty Ship of State
Staggers, bruised and torn and wounded by a derelict of fate,
One that drifted from its moorings in the anchorage of hate.

On the deck our noble Pilot, in the glory of his prime,
Lies in woe-impelling silence, dead before his hour or time,
Victim of a mind self-centred in a Godless fool of crime.

One of earth's dissension-breeders, one of Hate's unreasoning tools,
In the annals of the ages, when the world's hot anger cools,
He who sought for Crime's distinction shall be known as Chief of
    Fools.

In the annals of the ages, he who had no thought of fame
(Keeping on the path of duty, caring not for praise or blame),
Close beside the deathless Lincoln, writ in light, will shine his name.

Youth proclaimed him as a hero; time, a statesman; love, a man;
Death has crowned him as a martyr,—so from goal to goal he ran,
Knowing all the sum of glory that a human life may span.

He was chosen by the people; not an accident of birth
Made him ruler of a nation, but his own intrinsic worth.
Fools may govern over kingdoms—not republics of the earth.

He has raised the lovers' standard by his loyalty and faith,
He has shown how virile manhood may keep free from scandal's
    breath.
He has gazed, with trust unshaken, in the awful eyes of Death.

In the mighty march of progress he has sought to do his best.
Let his enemies be silent, as we lay him down to rest,
And may God assuage the anguish of one suffering woman's breast.

GRIEF

As the funeral train with its honoured dead
    On its mournful way went sweeping,
While a sorrowful nation bowed its head
    And the whole world joined in weeping,
I thought, as I looked on the solemn sight,
    Of the one fond heart despairing,
And I said to myself, as in truth I might,
    "How sad must be this *sharing*."

To share the living with even Fame,
    For a heart that is only human,
Is hard, when Glory asserts her claim
    Like a bold, insistent woman;
Yet a great, grand passion can put aside
    Or stay each selfish emotion,
And watch, with a pleasure that springs from pride,
    Its rival—the world's devotion.

But Death should render to love its own,
    And my heart bowed down and sorrowed
For the stricken woman who wept alone
    While even her *dead* was borrowed;

Borrowed from her, the bride—the wife—
　　For the world's last martial honour,
As she sat in the gloom of her darkened life,
　　With her widow's grief fresh upon her.

He had shed the glory of Love and Fame
　　In a golden halo about her;
She had shared his triumphs and worn his name:
　　But, alas! he had died without her.
He had wandered in many a distant realm,
　　And never had left her behind him,
But now, with a spectral shape at the helm,
　　He had sailed where she could not find him.

It was only a thought, that came that day
　　In the midst of the muffled drumming
And funeral music and sad display,
　　That I knew was right and becoming
Only a thought as the mourning train
　　Moved, column after column,
Bearing the dead to the burial plain
　　With a reverence grand as solemn.

ILLUSION

God and I in space alone
    And nobody else in view.
"And where are the people, O Lord," I said,
"The earth below, and the sky o'er head,
    And the dead whom once I knew?"

"That was a dream," God smiled and said—
    "A dream that seemed to be true.
There were no people, living or dead,
There was no earth, and no sky o'erhead;
    There was only Myself—in you."

"Why do I feel no fear," I asked,
    "Meeting You here this way?
For I have sinned I know full well?
And is there heaven, and is there hell,
    And is this the judgment day?"

"Say, those were but dreams," the Great God said,
    "Dreams, that have ceased to be.
There are no such things as fear or sin,
There is no you—you never have been—
    There is nothing at all but *Me*."

ASSERTION

I am serenity. Though passions beat
    Like mighty billows on my helpless heart,
I know beyond them lies the perfect sweet
    Serenity, which patience can impart.
And when wild tempests in my bosom rage,
"Peace, peace," I cry, "it is my heritage."

I am good health. Though fevers rack my brain
    And rude disorders mutilate my strength,
A perfect restoration after pain,
    I know shall be my recompense at length.
And so through grievous day and sleepless night,
"Health, health," I cry, "it is my own by right."

I am success. Though hungry, cold, ill-clad,
    I wander for awhile, I smile and say,
"It is but for a time—I shall be glad
    Tomorrow, for good fortune comes my way.
God is my father, He has wealth untold,
His wealth is mine, health, happiness, and gold."

I AM

I know not whence I came,
    I know not whither I go;
But the fact stands clear that I am here
    In this world of pleasure and woe.
And out of the mist and murk
    Another truth shines plain—
It is my power each day and hour
    To add to its joy or its pain.

I know that the earth exists,
    It is none of my business why;
I cannot find out what it's all about,
    I would but waste time to try.
My life is a brief, brief thing,
    I am here for a little space,
And while I stay I would like, if I may,
    To brighten and better the place.

The trouble, I think, with us all
    Is the lack of a high conceit.
If each man thought he was sent to this spot
    To make it a bit more sweet,

How soon we could gladden the world,
    How easily right all wrong,
If nobody shirked, and each one worked
    To help his fellows along!

Cease wondering why you came—
    Stop looking for faults and flaws;
Rise up today in your pride and say,
    "I am part of the First Great Cause!
However full the world,
    There is room for an earnest man.
It had need of me, or I would not be—
    I am here to strengthen the plan."

WISHING

Do you wish the world were better?
    Let me tell you what to do:
Set a watch upon your actions,
    Keep them always straight and true;
Rid your mind of selfish motives;
    Let your thoughts be clean and high.
You can make a little Eden
    Of the sphere you occupy.

Do you wish the world were wiser?
    Well, suppose you make a start,
By accumulating wisdom
    In the scrapbook of your heart:
Do not waste one page on folly;
    Live to learn, and learn to live.
If you want to give men knowledge
    You must get it, ere you give.

Do you wish the world were happy?
    Then remember day by day
Just to scatter seeds of kindness
    As you pass along the way;

For the pleasures of the many
    May be ofttimes traced to one,
As the hand that plants an acorn
    Shelters armies from the sun.

WE TWO

We two make home of any place we go;
We two find joy in any kind of weather;
    Or if the earth is clothed in bloom or snow,
    If summer days invite, or bleak winds blow,
What matters it if we two are together?
We two, we two, we make our world, our weather.

We two make banquets of the plainest fare;
In every cup we find the thrill of pleasure;
    We hide with wreaths the furrowed brow of care,
    And win to smiles the set lips of despair.
For us life always moves with lilting measure;
We two, we two, we make our world, our pleasure.

We two find youth renewed with every dawn;
Each day holds something of an unknown glory.
    We waste no thought on grief or pleasure gone;
    Tricked out like hope, time leads us on and on,
And thrums upon his harp new song or story.
We two, we two, we find the paths of glory.

We two make heaven here on this little earth;
We do not need to wait for realms eternal.
    We know the use of tears, know sorrow's worth,
    And pain for us is always love's rebirth.
Our paths lead closely by the paths supernal;
We two, we two, we live in love eternal.

THE POET'S THEME

What is the explanation of the strange silence of American poets
   concerning American triumphs on sea and land?
Literary Digest.

Why should the poet of these pregnant times
Be asked to sing of war's unholy crimes?

To laud and eulogize the trade which thrives
On horrid holocausts of human lives?

Man was a fighting beast when earth was young,
And war the only theme when Homer sung.

'Twixt might and might the equal contest lay,
Not so the battles of our modern day.

Too often now the conquering hero struts
A Gulliver among the Liliputs.

Success no longer rests on skill or fate,
But on the movements of a syndicate.

Of old men fought and deemed it right and just.
Today the warrior fights because he must,

And in his secret soul feels shame because
He desecrates the higher manhood's laws

Oh! there are worthier themes for poet's pen
In this great hour, than bloody deeds of men

Or triumphs of one hero (though he be
Deserving song for his humility):

The rights of many—not the worth of one;
The coming issues—not the battle done;

The awful opulence, and awful need;
The rise of brotherhood—the fall of greed,

The soul of man replete with God's own force,
The call "to heights," and not the cry "to horse,"—

Are there not better themes in this great age
For pen of poet, or for voice of sage

Than those old tales of killing? Song is dumb
Only that greater song in time may come.

When comes the bard, he whom the world waits for,
He will not sing of War.

SONG OF THE SPIRIT

All the aim of life is just
      Getting back to God.
Spirit casting off its dust,
      Getting back to God.
Every grief we have to bear
Disappointment, cross, despair
Each is but another stair
      Climbing back to God.

Step by step and mile by mile—
      Getting back to God;
Nothing else is worth the while—
      Getting back to God.
Light and shadow fill each day
Joys and sorrows pass away,
Smile at all, and smiling, say,
      Getting back to God.

Do not wear a mournful face
      Getting back to God;
Scatter sunshine on the place
      Going back to God;

Take what pleasure you can find,
But where'er your paths may wind.
Keep the purpose well in mind,—
        Getting back to God.

WOMANHOOD

She must be honest, both in thought and deed,
Of generous impulse, and above all greed;
Not seeking praise, or place, or power, or pelf,
But life's best blessings for her higher self,
Which means the best for all.
  She must have faith,
To make good friends of Trouble, Pain, and Death,
And understand their message.
  She should be
As redolent with tender sympathy
As is a rose with fragrance.
  Cheerfulness
Should be her mantle, even though her dress
May be of Sorrow's weaving.
  On her face
A loyal nature leaves its seal of grace,
And chastity is in her atmosphere.
Not that chill chastity which seems austere
(Like untrod snow-peaks, lovely to behold
Till once attained—then barren, loveless, cold);

But the white flame that feeds upon the soul
And lights the pathway to a peaceful goal.
A sense of humour, and a touch of mirth,
To brighten up the shadowy spots of earth;
And pride that passes evil—choosing good.
All these unite in perfect womanhood.

MORNING PRAYER

Let me today do something that shall take
    A little sadness from the world's vast store,
And may I be so favoured as to make
    Of joy's too scanty sum a little more
Let me not hurt, by any selfish deed
    Or thoughtless word, the heart of foe or friend;
Nor would I pass, unseeing, worthy need,
    Or sin by silence when I should defend.
However meagre be my worldly wealth,
    Let me give something that shall aid my. kind—
A word of courage, or a thought of health,
    Dropped as I pass for troubled hearts to find.
Let me tonight look back across the span
    'Twixt dawn and dark, and to my conscience say—
Because of some good act to beast or man—
    "The world is better that I lived today."

THE VOICES OF THE PEOPLE

Oh! I hear the people calling through the day time and the night time,
They are calling, they are crying for the coming of the right time.
It behooves you, men and women, it behooves you to be heeding,
For there lurks a note of menace underneath their plaintive pleading.

Let the land usurpers listen, let the greedy-hearted ponder,
On the meaning of the murmur, rising here and swelling yonder,
Swelling louder, waxing stronger, like a storm-fed stream that courses
Through the valleys, down abysses, growing, gaining with new forces.

Day by day the river widens, that great river of opinion,
And its torrent beats and plunges at the base of greed's dominion.
Though you dam it by oppression and fling golden bridges o'er it,
Yet the day and hour advances when in fright you'll flee before it.

Yes, I hear the people calling, through the night time and the day time,
Wretched toilers in life's autumn, weary young ones in life's May time—
They are crying, they are calling for their share of work and pleasure;
You are heaping high your coffers while you give them scanty
    measure,—
You have stolen God's wide acres, just to glut your swollen purses—
Oh! restore them to His children ere their pleading turns to curses.

THE WORLD GROWS BETTER

Oh! the earth is full of sinning
    And of trouble and of woe,
But the devil makes an inning
    Every time we say it's so.
And the way to set him scowling,
    And to put him back a pace,
Is to stop this stupid growling,
    And to look things in the face.

If you glance at history's pages,
    In all lands and eras known,
You will find the buried ages
    Far more wicked than our own.
As you scan each word and letter.
    You will realise it more,
That the world today is better
    Than it ever was before.

There is much that needs amending
    In the present time, no doubt;
There is right that needs amending,
    There is wrong needs crushing out.

And we hear the groans and curses
    Of the poor who starve and die,
While the men with swollen purses
    In the place of hearts go by.

But in spite of all the trouble
    That obscures the sun today,
Just remember it was double
    In the ages passed away.
And those wrongs shall all be righted,
    Good shall dominate the land,
For the darkness now is lighted
    By the torch in Science's hand.

Forth from little motes in Chaos,
    We have come to what we are;
And no evil force can stay us—
    We shall mount from star to star,
We shall break each bond and fetter
    That has bound us heretofore;
And the earth is surely better
    Than it ever was before.

A MAN'S IDEAL

A lovely little keeper of the home,
Absorbed in menu books, yet erudite
When I need counsel; quick at repartee
And slow to anger. Modest as a flower,
Yet scintillant and radiant as a star.
Unmercenary in her mould of mind,
While opulent and dainty in her tastes.
A nature generous and free, albeit
The incarnation of economy.
She must be chaste as proud Diana was,
Yet warm as Venus. To all others cold
As some white glacier glittering in the sun;
To me as ardent as the sensuous rose
That yields its sweetness to the burrowing bee
All ignorant of evil in the world,
And innocent as any cloistered nun,
Yet wise as Phryne in the arts of love
When I come thirsting to her nectared lips.
Good as the best, and tempting as the worst,
A saint, a siren, and a paradox.

THE FIRE BRIGADE

Hark! high o'er the rattle and clamour and clatter
    Of traffic-filled streets, do you hear that loud noise?
And pushing and rushing to see what's the matter,
    Like herds of wild cattle, go pell-mell the boys.

There's a fire in the city! the engines are coming!
    The bold bells are clanging, "Make way in the street!"
The wheels of the hose-cart are spinning and humming
    In time to the music of galloping feet.

Make way there! make way there! the horses are flying,
    The sparks from their swift hoofs shoot higher and higher,
The crowds are increasing—the gamins are crying:
    "Hooray, boys!" "Hooray, boys!" "Come on to the fire!"

With clanging and banging and clatter and rattle
    The long ladders follow the engine and hose.
The men are all ready to dash into battle;
    But will they come out again? God only knows.

At windows and doorways crowd questioning faces;
    There's something about it that quickens one's breath.
How proudly the brave fellows sit in their places—
    And speed to the conflict that may be their death!

Still faster and faster and faster and faster
        The grand horses thunder and leap on their way
The red foe is yonder, and may prove the master;
        Turn out there, bold traffic—turn out there, I say!

For once the loud truckman knows oaths will not matter
        And reins in his horses and yields to his fate.
The engines are coming! let pleasure-crowds scatter,
        Let street car and truckman and mail waggon wait.

They speed like a comet—they pass in a minute;
        The boys follow on like a tail to a kite;
The commonplace street has but traffic now in it—
        The great fire engines have swept out of sight.

THE TIDES

Be careful what rubbish you toss in the tide.
 On outgoing billows it drifts from your sight,
But back on the incoming waves it may ride
 And land at your threshold again before night.
Be careful what rubbish you toss in the tide.

Be careful what follies you toss in life's sea.
 On bright dancing billows they drift far away,
But back on the Nemesis tides they may be
 Thrown down at your threshold an unwelcome day
Be careful what follies you toss in youth's sea.

WHEN THE REGIMENT CAME BACK

All the uniforms were blue, all the swords were bright and new,
    When the regiment went marching down the street,
All the men were hale and strong as they proudly moved along,
    Through the cheers that drowned the music of their feet.
Oh the music of the feet keeping time to drums that beat,
    Oh the splendour and the glitter of the sight,
As with swords and rifles new and in uniforms of blue
    The regiment went marching to the fight!

When the regiment came back all the guns and swords were black
    And the uniforms had faded out to gray,
And the faces of the men who marched through that street again
    Seemed like faces of the dead who lose their way.
For the dead who lose their way cannot look more wan and gray.
    Oh the sorrow and the pity of the sight,
Oh the weary lagging feet out of step with drums that beat,
    As the regiment comes marching from the fight.

WOMAN TO MAN

Woman is man's enemy, rival, and competitor.—JOHN. J. INGALLS.

You do but jest, sir, and you jest not well,
How could the hand be enemy of the arm,
Or seed and sod be rivals! How could light
Feel jealousy of heat, plant of the leaf,
Or competition dwell 'twixt lip and smile?
Are we not part and parcel of yourselves?
Like strands in one great braid we entertwine
And make the perfect whole. You could not be,
Unless we gave you birth; we are the soil
From which you sprang, yet sterile were that soil
Save as you planted. (Though in the Book we read
One woman bore a child with no man's aid,
We find no record of a man-child born
Without the aid of woman! Fatherhood
Is but a small achievement at the best,
While motherhood comprises heaven and hell.)
This ever-growing argument of sex
Is most unseemly, and devoid of sense.
Why waste more time in controversy, when
There is not time enough for all of love,
Our rightful occupation in this life?
Why prate of our defects, of where we fail,
When just the story of our worth would need

Eternity for telling, and our best
Development comes ever through your praise,
As through our praise you reach your highest self?
Oh! had you not been miser of your praise
And let our virtues be their own reward,
The old-established order of the world
Would never have been changed. Small blame is ours
For this unsexing of ourselves, and worse.
Effeminising of the male. We were
Content, sir, till you starved us, heart and brain.
All we have done, or wise, or otherwise,
Traced to the root, was done for love of you.
Let us taboo all vain comparisons,
And go forth as God meant us, hand in hand,
Companions, mates, and comrades evermore;
Two parts of one divinely ordained whole.

THE TRAVELLER

Reply to Rudyard Kipling's "He travels the fastest who travels alone."

Who travels alone with his eyes on the heights,
Though he laughs in the day time oft weeps in the nights;

For courage goes down at the set of the sun,
When the toil of the journey is all borne by one.

He speeds but to grief though full gaily he ride
Who travels alone without love at his side.

Who travels alone without lover or friend
But hurries from nothing, to naught at the end.

Though great be his winnings and high be his goal,
He is bankrupt in wisdom and beggared in soul.

Life's one gift of value to him is denied
Who travels alone without love at his side.

It is easy enough in this world to make haste
If one live for that purpose—but think of the waste;

For life is a poem to leisurely read,
And the joy of the journey lies not in its speed.

Oh! vain his achievement and petty his pride
Who travels alone without love at his side.

THE EARTH

The earth is yours and mine,
    Our God's bequest.
That testament divine
    Who dare contest?

Usurpers of the earth,
    We claim our share.
We are of royal birth.
    Beware! beware!

Unloose the hand of greed
    From God's fair land,
We claim but what we need—
    That, we demand.

NOW

I leave with God tomorrow's where and how,
And do concern myself but with the Now,
That little word, though half the future's length,
Well used, holds twice its meaning and its strength.

Like one blindfolded groping out his way,
I will not try to touch beyond today.
Since all the future is concealed from sight
I need but strive to make the next step right.

That done, the next, and so on, till I find
Perchance some day I am no longer blind,
And looking up, behold a radiant Friend
Who says, "Rest, now, for you have reached the end."

YOU AND TODAY

With every rising of the sun
Think of your life as just begun.

The past has shrived and buried deep
All yesterdays—there let them sleep,

Nor seek to summon back one ghost
Of that innumerable host.

Concern yourself with but today;
Woo it and teach it to obey

Your wish and will. Since time began
Today has been the friend of man.

But in his blindness and his sorrow
He looks to yesterday and tomorrow.

You and today! a soul sublime
And the great pregnant hour of time.

With God between to bind the train,
Go forth, I say—attain—attain.

THE REASON

Do you know what moves the tides
    As they swing from low to high?
'Tis the love, love, love,
    Of the moon within the sky.
Oh! they follow where she guides,
Do the faithful-hearted tides.

Do you know what moves the earth
    Out of winter into spring?
'Tis the love, love, love,
    Of the sun, the mighty king.
Oh the rapture that finds birth
In the kiss of sun and earth!

Do you know what makes sweet songs
    Ring for me above earth's strife?
'Tis the love, love, love,
    That you bring into my life,
Oh the glory of the songs
In the heart where love belongs!

MISSION

If you are sighing for a lofty work,
    If great ambitions dominate your mind,
Just watch yourself and see you do not shirk
    The common little ways of being kind.

If you are dreaming of a future goal,
    When, crowned with glory, men shall own your power,
Be careful that you let no struggling soul
    Go by unaided in the present hour.

If you are moved to pity for the earth,
    And long to aid it, do not look so high,
You pass some poor, dumb creature faint with thirst—
    All life is equal in the eternal eye.

If you would help to make the wrong things right,
    Begin at home: there lies a lifetime's toil.
Weed your own garden fair for all men's sight,
    Before you plan to till another's soil.

God chooses His own leaders in the world,
    And from the rest He asks but willing hands.
As mighty mountains into place are hurled,
    While patient tides may only shape the sands.

REPETITION

Over and over and over
    These truths I will weave in song—
That God's great plan needs you and me,
That will is greater than destiny,
    And that love moves the world along.

However mankind may doubt it,
    It shall listen and hear my creed—
That God may ever be found within,
That the worship of self is the only sin,
    And the only devil is greed.

Over and over and over
    These truths I will say and sing,
That love is mightier far than hate,
That a man's own thought is a man's own fate,
    And that life is a goodly thing.

BEGIN THE DAY

Begin each morning with a talk to God,
And ask for your divine inheritance
Of usefulness, contentment, and success.
Resign all fear, all doubt, and all despair.
The stars doubt not, and they are undismayed,
Though whirled through space for countless centuries,
And told not why or wherefore: and the sea
With everlasting ebb and flow obeys,
And leaves the purpose with the unseen Cause.
The star sheds radiance on a million worlds,
The sea is prodigal with waves, and yet
No lustre from the star is lost, and not
One drop is missing from the ocean tides.
Oh! brother to the star and sea, know all
God's opulence is held in trust for those
Who wait serenely and who work in faith.

WORDS

Words are great forces in the realm of life:
    Be careful of their use. Who talks of hate,
Of poverty, of sickness, but sets rife
    These very elements to mar his fate.

When love, health, happiness, and plenty hear
    Their names repeated over day by day,
They wing their way like answering fairies near,
    Then nestle down within our homes to stay.

Who talks of evil conjures into shape
    The formless thing and gives it life and scope.
This is the law: then let no word escape
    That does not breathe of everlasting hope.

FATE AND I

Wise men tell me thou, O Fate,
Art invincible and great.

Well, I own thy prowess; still
Dare I flout thee with my will

Thou canst shatter in a span
All the earthly pride of man.

Outward things thou canst control;
But stand back—I rule my soul!

Death? 'Tis such a little thing—
Scarcely worth the mentioning.

What has death to do with me,
Save to set my spirit free?

Something in me dwells, O Fate,
That can rise and dominate

Loss, and sorrow, and disaster,—
How, then, Fate, art thou my master?

In the great primeval morn
My immortal will was born,

Part of that stupendous Cause
Which conceived the Solar Laws,

Lit the suns and filled the seas,
Royalest of pedigrees.

That great Cause was Love, the Source
Who most loves has most of Force.

He who harbours Hate one hour
Saps the soul of Peace and Power.

He who will not hate his foe
Need not dread life's hardest blow.

In the realm of brotherhood
Wishing no man aught but good,

Naught but good can come to me—
This is Love's supreme decree.

Since I bar my door to Hate,
What have I to fear, O Fate?

Since I fear not—Fate I vow,
I the ruler am, not thou!

ATTAINMENT

Use all your hidden forces. Do not miss
The purpose of this life, and do not wait
For circumstance to mould or change your fate;
In your own self lies Destiny. Let this
Vast truth cast out all fear, all prejudice,
All hesitation. Know that you are great,
Great with divinity. So dominate
Environment, and enter into bliss.
Love largely and hate nothing. Hold no aim
That does not chord with universal good.
Hear what the voices of the Silence say—
All joys are yours if you put forth your claim.
Once let the spiritual laws be understood,
Material things must answer and obey.

A PLEA TO PEACE

When mighty issues loom before us, all
The petty great men of the day seem small,
Like pigmies standing in a blaze of light
Before some grim majestic mountain-height.
War, with its bloody and impartial hand,
Reveals the hidden weakness of a land,
Uncrowns the heroes trusting Peace has made
Of men whose honour is a thing of trade,
And turns the searchlight full on many a place
Where proud conventions long have masked disgrace.
O lovely Peace! as thou art fair be wise.
Demand great men, and great men shall arise
To do thy bidding. Even as warriors come,
Swift at the call of bugle and of drum,
So at the voice of Peace, imperative
As bugle's call, shall heroes spring to live
For country and for thee. In every land,
In every age, men are what times demand.
Demand the best, O Peace, and teach thy sons
They need not rush in front of death-charged guns
With murder in their hearts to prove their worth.
The grandest heroes who have graced the earth
Were love-filled souls who did not seek the fray,

But chose the safe, hard, high, and lonely way
Of selfless labour for a suffering world.
Beneath our glorious flag again unfurled
In victory such heroes wait to be
Called into bloodless action, Peace, by thee.
Be thou insistent in thy stern demand,
And wise, great men shall rise up in the land.

PRESUMPTION

Whenever I am prone to doubt or wonder—
    I check myself, and say, "That mighty One
Who made the solar system cannot blunder—
    And for the best all things are being done."
Who set the stars on their eternal courses
    Has fashioned this strange earth by some sure plan.
Bow low, bow low to those majestic forces,
    Nor dare to doubt their wisdom, puny man.

You cannot put one little star in motion,
    You cannot shape one single forest leaf,
Nor fling a mountain up, nor sink an ocean,
    Presumptuous pigmy, large with unbelief.
You cannot bring one dawn of regal splendour,
    Nor bid the day to shadowy twilight fall,
Nor send the pale moon forth with radiance tender—
    And dare you doubt the One who has done all?

"So much is wrong, there is such pain—such sinning."
    Yet look again—behold how much is right!
And He who formed the world from its beginning
    Knows how to guide it upward to the light.

Your task, O man, is not to carp and cavil
    At God's achievements, but with purpose strong
To cling to good, and turn away from evil.
    That is the way to help the world along.

HIGH NOON

Time's finger on the dial of my life
Points to high noon! and yet the half-spent day
Leaves less than half remaining, for the dark,
Bleak shadows of the grave engulf the end.
To those who burn the candle to the stick,
The sputtering socket yields but little light.
Long life is sadder than an early death.
We cannot count on ravelled threads of age
Whereof to weave a fabric. We must use
The warp and woof the ready present yields
And toil while daylight lasts. When I bethink
How brief the past, the future, still more brief
Calls on to action, action! Not for me
Is time for retrospection or for dreams,
Not time for self-laudation or remorse.
Have I done nobly? Then I must not let
Dead yesterday unborn tomorrow shame.
Have I done wrong? Well, let the bitter taste
Of fruit that turned to ashes on my lip
Be my reminder in temptation's hour,
And keep me silent when I would condemn.
Sometimes it takes the acid of a sin
To cleanse the clouded windows of our souls
So pity may shine through them.

Looking back,
My faults and errors seem like stepping-stones
That led the way to knowledge of the truth
And made me value virtue; sorrows shine
In rainbow colours o'er the gulf of years,
Where lie forgotten pleasures.

  Looking forth,
Out to the western sky still bright with noon,
I feel well spurred and booted for the strife
That ends not till Nirvana is attained.

Battling with fate, with men, and with myself,
Up the steep summit of my life's forenoon,
Three things I learned, three things of precious worth,
To guide and help me down the western slope.
I have learned how to pray, and toil, and save:
To pray for courage to receive what comes,
Knowing what comes to be divinely sent;
To toil for universal good, since thus
And only thus can good come unto me;
To save, by giving whatsoe'er I have
To those who have not—this alone is gain.

THOUGHT-MAGNETS

With each strong thought, with every earnest longing
    For aught thou deemest needful to thy soul,
Invisible vast forces are set thronging
    Between thee and that goal

'Tis only when some hidden weakness alters
    And changes thy desire, or makes it less,
That this mysterious army ever falters
    Or stops short of success.

Thought is a magnet; and the longed-for pleasure,
    Or boon, or aim, or object, is the steel;
And its attainment hangs but on the measure
    Of what thy soul can feel.

SMILES

Smile a little, smile a little,
    As you go along,
Not alone when life is pleasant,
    But when things go wrong.
Care delights to see you frowning,
    Loves to hear you sigh;
Turn a smiling face upon her—
    Quick the dame will fly.

Smile a little, smile a little,
    All along the road;
Every life must have its burden,
    Every heart its load.
Why sit down in gloom and darkness
    With your grief to sup?
As you drink Fate's bitter tonic,
    Smile across the cup.

Smile upon the troubled pilgrims
    Whom you pass and meet;
Frowns are thorns, and smiles are blossoms
    Oft for weary feet.

Do not make the way seem harder
    By a sullen face;
Smile a little, smile a little,
    Brighten up the place.

Smile upon your undone labour;
    Not for one who grieves
O'er his task waits wealth or glory;
    He who smiles achieves.
Though you meet with loss and sorrow
    In the passing years,
Smile a little, smile a little,
    Even through your tears.

THE UNDISCOVERED COUNTRY

Man has explored all countries and all lands,
And made his own the secrets of each clime.
Now, ere the world has fully reached its prime,
The oval earth lies compassed with steel bands,
The seas are slaves to ships that touch all strands,
    And even the haughty elements, sublime
    And bold, yield him their secrets for all time,
And speed like lackeys forth at his commands.

Still, though he search from shore to distant shore,
    And no strange realms, no unlocated plains
Are left for his attainment and control,
Yet is there one more kingdom to explore.
    Go, know thyself, O man! there yet remains
The undiscovered country of thy soul!

THE UNIVERSAL ROUTE

As we journey along, with a laugh and a song,
    We see, on youth's flower-decked slope,
Like a beacon of light, shining fair on the sight,
    The beautiful Station of Hope.

But the wheels of old Time roll along as we climb,
    And our youth speeds away on the years;
And with hearts that are numb with life's sorrows we come
    To the mist-covered Station of Tears.

Still onward we pass, where the milestones, alas!
    Are the tombs of our dead, to the West,
Where glitters and gleams, in the dying sunbeams,
    The sweet, silent Station of Rest.

All rest is but change, and no grave can estrange
    The soul from its Parent above;
And, scorning the rod, it soars back to its God,
    To the limitless City of Love.

UNANSWERED PRAYERS

Like some schoolmaster, kind in being stern,
Who hears the children crying o'er their slates
And calling, "Help me, master!" yet helps not,
Since in his silence and refusal lies
Their self-development, so God abides
Unheeding many prayers. He is not deaf
To any cry sent up from earnest hearts;
He hears and strengthens when He must deny.
He sees us weeping over life's hard sums;
But should He give the key and dry our tears,
What would it profit us when school were done
And not one lesson mastered?

    What a world
Were this if all our prayers were answered. Not
In famed Pandora's box were such vast ills
As lie in human hearts. Should our desires,
Voiced one by one in prayer, ascend to God
And come back as events shaped to our wish,
What chaos would result!

    In my fierce youth
I sighed out breath enough to move a fleet,
Voicing wild prayers to heaven for fancied boons
Which were denied; and that denial bends

My knee to prayers of gratitude each day
Of my maturer years. Yet from those prayers
I rose alway regirded for the strife
And conscious of new strength. Pray on, sad heart,
That which thou pleadest for may not be given,
But in the lofty altitude where souls
Who supplicate God's grace are lifted, there
Thou shalt find help to bear thy daily lot
Which is not elsewhere found.

THANKSGIVING

We walk on starry fields of white
    And do not see the daisies,
For blessings common in our sight
    We rarely offer praises.
We sigh for some supreme delight
    To crown our lives with splendour,
And quite ignore our daily store
    Of pleasures sweet and tender.

Our cares are bold and push their way
    Upon our thought and feeling;
They hang about us all the day,
    Our time from pleasure stealing.
So unobtrusive many a joy
    We pass by and forget it,
But worry strives to own our lives,
    And conquers if we let it.

There's not a day in all the year
    But holds some hidden pleasure,
And, looking back, joys oft appear
    To brim the past's wide measure.

But blessings are like friends, I hold,
　　　Who love and labour near us.
We ought to raise our notes of praise
　　　While living hearts can hear us.

Full many a blessing wears the guise
　　　Of worry or of trouble;
Far-seeing is the soul, and wise,
　　　Who knows the mask is double.
But he who has the faith and strength
　　　To thank his God for sorrow
Has found a joy without alloy
　　　To gladden every morrow.

We ought to make the moments notes
　　　Of happy, glad Thanksgiving;
The hours and days a silent phrase
　　　Of music we are living.
And so the theme should swell and grow
　　　As weeks and months pass o'er us,
And rise sublime at this good time,
　　　A grand Thanksgiving chorus.

CONTRASTS

I see the tall church steeples—
    They reach so far, so far;
But the eyes of my heart see the world's great mart
Where the starving people are.

    I hear the church bells ringing
    Their chimes on the morning air;
But my soul's sad ear is hurt to hear
    The poor man's cry of despair.

Thicker and thicker the churches,
    Nearer and nearer the sky—
But alack for their creeds while the poor man's needs
    Grow deeper as years roll by!

THY SHIP

Hadst thou a ship, in whose vast hold lay stored
The priceless riches of all climes and lands,
Say, wouldst thou let it float upon the seas
Unpiloted, of fickle winds the sport,
And of wild waves and hidden rocks the prey?

Thine is that ship; and in its depths concealed
Lies all the wealth of this vast universe—
Yea, lies some part of God's omnipotence,
The legacy divine of every soul.
Thy will, O man, thy will is that great ship,
And yet behold it drifting here and there—
One moment lying motionless in port,
Then on high seas by sudden impulse flung,
Then drying on the sands, and yet again
Sent forth on idle quests to no-man's land
To carry nothing and to nothing bring;
Till, worn and fretted by the aimless strife
And buffeted by vacillating winds,
It founders on a rock, or springs a leak,
With all its unused treasures in the hold.

Go save thy ship, thou sluggard; take the wheel
And steer to knowledge, glory, and success.
Great mariners have made the pathway plain
For thee to follow; hold thou to the course

Of Concentration Channel, and all things
Shall come in answer to thy swerveless wish
As comes the needle to the magnet's call,
Or sunlight to the prisoned blade of grass
That yearns all winter for the kiss of spring.

LIFE

All in the dark we grope along,
    And if we go amiss
We learn at least which path is wrong,
    And there is gain in this.

We do not always win the race
    By only running right;
We have to tread the mountain's base
    Before we reach its height.

The Christs alone no errors made;
    So often had they trod
The paths that lead through light and shade,
    They had become as God.

As Krishna, Buddha, Christ again,
    They passed along the way,
And left those mighty truths which men
    But dimly grasp today.

But he who loves himself the last
    And knows the use of pain,
Though strewn with errors all his past,
    He surely shall attain.

Some souls there are that needs must taste
    Of wrong, ere choosing right;
We should not call those years a waste
    Which led us to the light.

A MARINE ETCHING

A yacht from its harbour ropes pulled free,
And leaped like a steed o'er the race-track blue,
Then up behind her the dust of the sea,
A gray fog, drifted, and hid her from view.

"LOVE THYSELF LAST"

Love thyself last. Look near, behold thy duty
 To those who walk beside thee down life's road.
Make glad their days by little acts of beauty
 And help them bear the burden of earth's load.

Love thyself last. Look far and find the stranger
 Who staggers 'neath his sin and his despair;
Go, lend a hand, and lead him out of danger,
 To heights where he may see the world is fair.

Love thyself last. The vastnesses above thee
 Are filled with Spirit-Forces; strong and pure
And fervently these faithful friends shall love thee
 Keep thou thy watch o'er others and endure.

Love thyself last, and oh! such joy shall thrill thee
 As never yet to selfish souls was given;
Whate'er thy lot, a perfect peace will fill thee,
 And earth shall seem the ante-room of Heaven.

Love thyself last, and thou shalt grow in spirit
 To see, to hear, to know, and understand.
The message of the stars, lo, thou shalt hear it,
 And all God's joys shall be at thy command.

CHRISTMAS FANCIES

When Christmas bells are swinging above the fields of snow,
We hear sweet voices ringing from lands of long ago,
    And etched on vacant places
    Are half-forgotten faces
Of friends we used to cherish, and loves we used to know—
When Christmas bells are swinging above the fields of snow.

Uprising from the ocean of the present surging near,
We see, with strange emotion, that is not free from fear,
    That continent Elysian
    Long vanished from our vision,
Youth's lovely lost Atlantis, so mourned for and so dear,
Uprising from the ocean of the present surging near.

When gloomy, gray Decembers are roused to Christmas mirth,
The dullest life remembers there once was joy on earth,
    And draws from youth's recesses
    Some memory it possesses,
And, gazing through the lens of time, exaggerates its worth,
When gloomy, gray December is roused to Christmas mirth.

When hanging up the holly or mistletoe, I wis
Each heart recalls some folly that lit the world with bliss.
    Not all the seers and sages
    With wisdom of the ages

Can give the mind such pleasure as memories of that kiss
When hanging up the holly or mistletoe, I wis.

For life was made for loving, and love alone repays,
As passing years are proving, for all of Time's sad ways.
    There lies a sting in pleasure,
    And fame gives shallow measure,
And wealth is but a phantom that mocks the restless days,
For life was made for loving, and only loving pays.

When Christmas bells are pelting the air with silver chimes,
And silences are melting to soft, melodious rhymes,
    Let Love, the world's beginning,
    End fear and hate and sinning;
Let Love, the God Eternal, be worshipped in all climes
When Christmas bells are pelting the air with silver chimes.

THE RIVER

I am a river flowing from God's sea
Through devious ways. He mapped my course for me;
I cannot change it; mine alone the toil
To keep the waters free from grime and soil.
The winding river ends where it began;
And when my life has compassed its brief span
I must return to that mysterious source.
So let me gather daily on my course
The perfume from the blossoms as I pass,
Balm from the pines, and healing from the grass,
And carry down my current as I go
Not common stones but precious gems to show;
And tears (the holy water from sad eyes)
Back to God's sea, from which all rivers rise,
Let me convey, not blood from wounded hearts,
Nor poison which the upas tree imparts.
When over flowery vales I leap with joy,
Let me not devastate them, nor destroy,
But rather leave them fairer to the sight;
Mine be the lot to comfort and delight.
And if down awful chasms I needs must leap,

Let me not murmur at my lot, but sweep
On bravely to the end without one fear,
Knowing that He who planned my ways stands near.
Love sent me forth, to Love I go again,
For Love is all, and over all. Amen.

SORRY

There is much that makes me sorry as I journey down life's way,
And I seem to see more pathos in poor human lives each day.
I'm sorry for the strong, brave men who shield the weak from harm,
But who, in their own troubled hours, find no protecting arm.

I'm sorry for the victors who have reached success, to stand
As targets for the arrows shot by envious failure's hand.
I'm sorry for the generous hearts who freely shared their wine,
But drink alone the gall of tears in fortune's drear decline.

I'm sorry for the souls who build their own fame's funeral pyre,
Derided by the scornful throng like ice deriding fire.
I'm sorry for the conquering ones who know not sin's defeat,
But daily tread down fierce desire 'neath scorched and bleeding feet.

I'm sorry for the anguished hearts that break with passion's strain,
But I'm sorrier for the poor starved souls that never knew love's pain,
Who hunger on through barren years not tasting joys they crave,
For sadder far is such a lot than weeping o'er a grave.

I'm sorry for the souls that come unwelcomed into birth,
I'm sorry for the unloved old who cumber up the earth,
I'm sorry for the suffering poor in life's great maelstrom hurled—
In truth, I'm sorry for them all who make this aching world.

But underneath whate'er seems sad and is not understood,
I know there lies hid from our sight a mighty germ of good.
And this belief stands firm by me, my sermon, motto, text—
The sorriest things in this life will seem grandest in the next.

AMBITION'S TRAIL

If all the end of this continuous striving
    Were simply *to attain*,
How poor would seem the planning and contriving,
The endless urging and the hurried driving,
    Of body, heart, and brain!

But ever in the wake of true achieving
    There shines this glowing trail—
Some other soul will be spurred on, conceiving
New strength and hope, in its own power believing,
    Because *thou* didst not fail.

Not thine alone the glory, nor the sorrow,
    If thou dost miss the goal;
Undreamed of lives in many a far tomorrow
From thee their weakness or their force shall borrow—
    On, on, ambitious soul.

UNCONTROLLED

The mighty forces of mysterious space
    Are one by one subdued by lordly man.
    The awful lightning that for eons ran
    Their devastating and untrammelled race,
Now bear his messages from place to place
    Like carrier doves. The winds lead on his van;
    The lawless elements no longer can
Resist his strength, but yield with sullen grace.

His bold feet scaling heights before untrod,
    Light, darkness, air and water, heat and cold,
    He bids go forth and bring him power and pelf.
And yet, though ruler, king and demi-god,
    He walks with his fierce passions uncontrolled,
    The conqueror of all things—save himself.

WILL

You will be what you will to be;
    Let failure find its false content
    In that poor word "environment,"
But spirit scorns it, and is free.

It masters time, it conquers space,
    It cowes that boastful trickster Chance,
    And bids the tyrant Circumstance
Uncrown and fill a servant's place.

The human Will, that force unseen,
    The offspring of a deathless Soul,
    Can hew the way to any goal,
Though walls of granite intervene.

Be not impatient in delay,
    But wait as one who understands;
    When spirit rises and commands,
The gods are ready to obey.

The river seeking for the sea
    Confronts the dam and precipice,
    Yet knows it cannot fail or miss;
You will be what you will to be!

TO AN ASTROLOGER

Nay, seer, I do not doubt thy mystic lore,
Nor question that the tenor of my life,
Past, present, and the future, is revealed
There in my horoscope. I do believe
That yon dead moon compels the haughty seas
To ebb and flow, and that my natal star
Stands like a stern-browed sentinel in space
And challenges events; nor lets one grief,
Or joy, or failure, or success, pass on
To mar or bless my earthly lot, until
It proves its Karmic right to come to me.

All this I grant, but more than this I *know*!
Before the solar systems were conceived,
When nothing was but the unnamable,
My spirit lived, an atom of the Cause.
Through countless ages and in many forms
It has existed, ere it entered in
This human frame to serve its little day
Upon the earth. The deathless Me of me.
The spark from that great all-creative fire,
Is part of that eternal source called God,
And mightier than the universe.

           Why, he
Who knows, and knowing, never once forgets
The pedigree divine of his own soul,
Can conquer, shape, and govern destiny,
And use vast space as 'twere a board for chess
With stars for pawns; can change his horoscope
To suit his will; turn failure to success,
And from preordained sorrows, harvest joy.

There is no puny planet, sun, or moon,
Or zodiacal sign which can control
The God in us! If we bring *that* to bear
Upon events, we mould them to our wish;
'Tis when the infinite 'neath the finite gropes
That men are governed by their horoscopes.

THE TENDRIL'S FATE

Under the snow, in the dark and the cold,
    A pale little sprout was humming;
Sweetly it sang, 'neath the frozen mould,
    Of the beautiful days that were coming.

"How foolish your songs!" said a lump of clay;
    "What is there, I ask, to prove them?
Just look at the walls between you and the day,
    Now, have you the strength to move them?"

But under the ice and under the snow
    The pale little sprout kept singing,
"I cannot tell how, but I know, I know,
    I know what the days are bringing.

"Birds, and blossoms, and buzzing bees,
    Blue, blue skies above me,
Bloom on the meadows and buds on the trees
    And the great glad sun to love me."

A pebble spoke next: "You are quite absurd,"
    It said, "with your song's insistence;
For *I* never saw a tree or a bird,
    So of course there are none in existence."

"But I know, I know," the tendril cried,
　　In beautiful sweet unreason;
Till lo! from its prison, glorified,
　　It burst in the glad spring season.

THE TIMES

The times are not degenerate. Man's faith
Mounts higher than of old. No crumbling creed
Can take from the immortal soul the need
　　Of that supreme Creator, God. The wraith
Of dead beliefs we cherished in our youth
Fades but to let us welcome new-born Truth.

　　Man may not worship at the ancient shrine
Prone on his face, in self-accusing scorn.
That night is past. He hails a fairer morn,
　　And knows himself a something all divine;
Not humble worm whose heritage is sin,
But, born of God, he feels the Christ withal.

　　Not loud his prayers, as in the olden time,
But deep his reverence for that mighty force,
That occult working of the great All-Source,
　　Which makes the present era so sublime.
Religion now means something high and broad.
And man stood never half so near to God.

THE QUESTION

Beside us in our seeking after pleasures,
    Through all our restless striving after fame,
Through all our search for worldly gains and treasures,
    There walketh one whom no man likes to name.
Silent he follows, veiled of form and feature,
    Indifferent if we sorrow or rejoice,
Yet that day comes when every living creature
    Must look upon his face and hear his voice.

When that day comes to you, and Death, unmasking,
    Shall bar your path, and say, "Behold the end,"
What are the questions that he will be asking
    About your past? Have you considered, friend?
I think he will not chide you for your sinning,
    Nor for your creeds or dogmas will he care;
He will but ask, "From your life's first beginning
    How many burdens have you helped to bear?"

SORROW'S USES

The uses of sorrow I comprehend
Better and better at each year's end.

Deeper and deeper I seem to see
Why and wherefore it has to be.

Only after the dark, wet days
Do we fully rejoice in the sun's bright rays.

Sweeter the crust tastes after the fast
Than the sated gourmand's finest repast.

The faintest cheer sounds never amiss
To the actor who once has heard a hiss.

To one who the sadness of freedom knows,
Light seem the fetters love may impose.

And he who has dwelt with his heart alone,
Hears all the music in friendship's tone.

So better and better I comprehend
How sorrow ever would be our friend.

IF

'Twixt what thou art, and what thou wouldst be, let
No "If" arise on which to lay the blame.
Man makes a mountain of that puny word,
But, like a blade of grass before the scythe,
It falls and withers when a human will,
Stirred by creative force, sweeps toward its aim.

Thou wilt be what thou couldst be. Circumstance
Is but the toy of genius. When a soul
Burns with a god-like purpose to achieve,
All obstacles between it and its goal
Must vanish as the dew before the sun.

"If" is the motto of the dilettante
And idle dreamer; 'tis the poor excuse
Of mediocrity. The truly great
Know not the word, or know it but to scorn,
Else had Joan of Arc a peasant died,
Uncrowned by glory and by men unsung.

WHICH ARE YOU?

There are two kinds of people on earth today;
Just two kinds of people, no more, I say.

Not the sinner and saint, for it's well understood
The good are half bad, and the bad are half good.

Not the rich and the poor, for to rate a man's wealth
You must first know the state of his conscience and health.

Not the humble and proud, for, in life's little span,
Who puts on vain airs is not counted a man.

Not the happy and sad, for the swift flying years
Bring each man his laughter, and each man his tears.

No; the two kinds of people on earth I mean
Are the people who lift, and the people who lean.

Wherever you go, you will find the earth's masses
Are always divided in just these two classes.

And, oddly enough, you will find too, I ween,
There's only one lifter to twenty who lean.

In which class are you? Are you easing the load
Of overtaxed lifters, who toil down the road?

Or are you a leaner, who lets others share
Your portion of labour and worry and care?

THE CREED TO BE

Our thoughts are moulding unmade spheres,
    And, like a blessing or a curse,
They thunder down the formless years,
    And ring throughout the universe.

We build our futures by the shape
    Of our desires, and not by acts.
There is no pathway of escape;
    No priest-made creeds can alter facts.

Salvation is not begged or bought;
    Too long this selfish hope sufficed;
Too long man reeked with lawless thought,
    And leaned upon a tortured Christ.

Like shrivelled leaves, these worn-out creeds
    Are dropping from Religion's tree;
The world begins to know its needs,
    And souls are crying to be free.

Free from the load of fear and grief,
    Man fashioned in an ignorant age;
Free from the ache of unbelief
    He fled to in rebellious rage.

No church can bind him to the things
    That fed the first crude souls, evolved;
For, mounting up on daring wings,
    He questions mysteries all unsolved.

Above the chant of priests, above
    The blatant voice of braying doubt,
He hears the still, small voice of Love,
    Which sends its simple message out.

And clearer, sweeter, day by day,
    Its mandate echoes from the skies,
"Go roll the stone of self away,
    And let the Christ within thee rise."

INSPIRATION

Not like a daring, bold, aggressive boy,
 Is inspiration, eager to pursue,
But rather like a maiden, fond, yet coy,
 Who gives herself to him who best doth woo.

Once she may smile, or thrice, thy soul to fire,
 In passing by, but when she turns her face,
Thou must persist and seek her with desire,
 If thou wouldst win the favour of her grace.

And if, like some winged bird, she cleaves the air,
 And leaves thee spent and stricken on the earth,
Still must thou strive to follow even there,
 That she may know thy valour and thy worth.

Then shall she come unveiling all her charms,
 Giving thee joy for pain, and smiles for tears;
Then shalt thou clasp her with possessing arms,
 The while she murmurs music in thine ears.

But ere her kiss has faded from thy cheek,
 She shall flee from thee over hill and glade,
So must thou seek and ever seek and seek
 For each new conquest of this phantom maid

THE WISH

Should some great angel say to me tomorrow,
 "Thou must re-tread thy pathway from the start,
But God will grant, in pity, for thy sorrow,
 Some one dear wish, the nearest to thy heart."

This were my wish!—from my life's dim beginning
 Let be what has been! wisdom planned the whole
My want, my woe, my errors, and my sinning,
 All, all were needed lessons for my soul.

THREE FRIENDS

Of all the blessings which my life has known,
I value most, and most praise God for three:
Want, Loneliness, and Pain, those comrades true,

Who masqueraded in the garb of foes
For many a year, and filled my heart with dread.
Yet fickle joys, like false, pretentious friends,
Have proved less worthy than this trio. First,

Want taught me labour, led me up the steep
And toilsome paths to hills of pure delight,
Trod only by the feet that know fatigue,
And yet press on until the heights appear.

Then loneliness and hunger of the heart
Sent me upreaching to the realms of space,
Till all the silences grew eloquent,
And all their loving forces hailed me friend.

Last, pain taught prayer! placed in my hand the staff
Of close communion with the over-soul,
That I might lean upon it to the end,
And find myself made strong for any strife.

And then these three who had pursued my steps
Like stern, relentless foes, year after year,
Unmasked, and turned their faces full on me,
And lo! they were divinely beautiful,
For through them shone the lustrous eyes of Love.

YOU NEVER CAN TELL

You never can tell when you send a word,
 Like an arrow shot from a bow
By an archer blind, be it cruel or kind,
 Just where it may chance to go!
It may pierce the breast of your dearest friend,
 Tipped with its poison or balm;
To a stranger's heart in life's great mart,
 It may carry its pain or its calm.

You never can tell when you do an act
 Just what the result will be;
But with every deed you are sowing a seed,
 Though the harvest you may not see.
Each kindly act is an acorn dropped
 In God's productive soil.
You may not know, but the tree shall grow,
 With shelter for those who toil.

You never can tell what your thoughts will do,
 In bringing you hate or love;
For thoughts are things, and their airy wings
 Are swifter than carrier doves.

They follow the law of the universe—
    Each thing must create its kind;
And they speed o'er the track to bring you back
    Whatever went out from your mind.

HERE AND NOW

Here, in the heart of the world,
    Here, in the noise and the din,
Here, where our spirits were hurled
    To battle with sorrow and sin,
This is the place and the spot
    For knowledge of infinite things
This is the kingdom where Thought
    Can conquer the prowess of kings

Wait for no heavenly life,
    Seek for no temple alone;
Here, in the midst of the strife,
    Know what the sages have known.
See what the Perfect Ones saw—
    God in the depth of each soul,
God as the light and the law,
    God as beginning and goal.

Earth is one chamber of Heaven,
    Death is no grander than birth.
Joy in the life that was given,
    Strive for perfection on earth;

Here, in the turmoil and roar,
    Show what it is to be calm;
Show how the spirit can soar
    And bring hack its healing and balm.

Stand not aloof nor apart,
    Plunge in the thick of the fight;
There, in the street and the mart,
    That is the place to do right.
Not in some cloister or cave,
    Not in some kingdom above,
Here, on this side of the grave,
    Here, should we labour and love.

UNCONQUERED

However skilled and strong art thou, my foe,
However fierce is thy relentless hate,
Though firm thy hand, and strong thy aim, and straight
Thy poisoned arrow leaves the bended bow,

To pierce the target of my heart, ah! know
    I am the master yet of my own fate.
    Thou canst not rob me of my best estate,
Though fortune, fame, and friends, yea, love shall go.

Not to the dust shall my true self be hurled,
    Nor shall I meet thy worst assaults dismayed;
    When all things in the balance are well weighed,
There is but one great danger in the world—
    Thou canst not force my soul to wish thee ill,
    That is the only evil that can kill.

ALL THAT LOVE ASKS

"All that I ask," says Love, "is just to stand
    And gaze, unchided, deep in thy dear eyes;
    For in their depths lies largest Paradise.
Yet, if perchance one pressure of thy hand
    Be granted me, then joy I thought complete
    Were still more sweet.

"All that I ask," says Love, "all that I ask,
    Is just thy hand-clasp. Could I brush thy cheek
    As zephyrs brush a rose leaf, words are weak
To tell the bliss in which my soul would bask.
    There is no language but would desecrate
    A joy so great.

"All that I ask, is just one tender touch
    Of that soft cheek. Thy pulsing palm in mine,
    Thy dark eyes lifted in a trust divine,
And those curled lips that tempt me overmuch
    Turned where I may not seize the supreme bliss
    Of one mad kiss.

"All that I ask," says Love, "of life, of death,
    Or of high heaven itself, is just to stand,
    Glance melting into glance, hand twined in hand,
The while I drink the nectar of thy breath

In one sweet kiss, but one, of all thy store,
    I ask no more."

"All that I ask"—nay, self-deceiving Love,
    Reverse thy phrase, so thus the words may fall,
    In place of "all I ask," say, "I ask all,"
All that pertains to earth or soars above,
    All that thou wert, art, will be, body, soul,
    Love asks the whole,

"DOES IT PAY?"

If one poor burdened toiler o'er life's road,
    Who meets us by the way,
Goes on less conscious of his galling load,
    Then life, indeed, does pay.

If we can show one troubled heart the gain
    That lies alway in loss,
Why, then, we too are paid for all the pain
    Of bearing life's hard cross.

If some despondent soul to hope is stirred,
    Some sad lip made to smile,
By any act of ours, or any word,
    Then, life has been worth while.

SESTINA

I wandered o'er the vast green plains of youth,
And searched for Pleasure. On a distant height
Fame's silhouette stood sharp against the skies.
Beyond vast crowds that thronged a broad highway
I caught the glimmer of a golden goal,
While from a blooming bower smiled siren Love.

Straight gazing in her eyes, I laughed at Love
With all the haughty insolence of youth,
As past her bower I strode to seek my goal.
"Now will I climb to glory's dizzy height,"
I said, "for there above the common way
Doth pleasure dwell companioned by the skies."

But when I reached that summit near the skies,
So far from man I seemed, so far from Love—
"Not here," I cried, "doth Pleasure find her way."
Seen from the distant borderland of youth,
Fame smiles upon us from her sun-kissed height,
But frowns in shadows when we reach the goal.

Then were mine eyes fixed on that glittering goal,
Dear to all sense—sunk souls beneath the skies.
Gold tempts the artist from the lofty height,

Gold lures the maiden from the arms of Love,
Gold buys the fresh, ingenuous heart of youth,
"And gold," I said, "will show me Pleasure's way."

But ah! the soil and discord of that way,
Where savage hordes rushed headlong to the goal,
Dead to the best impulses of their youth,
Blind to the azure beauty of the skies;
Dulled to the voice of conscience and of love,
They wandered far from Truth's eternal height.

Then Truth spoke to me from that noble height,
Saying, "Thou didst pass Pleasure on the way,
She with the yearning eyes so full of Love,
Whom thou disdained to seek for glory's goal.
Two blending paths beneath God's arching skies
Lead straight to Pleasure. Ah! blind heart of youth,
Not up fame's height, not toward the base god's goal,
Doth Pleasure make her way, but 'neath calm skies
Where Duty walks with Love in endless youth."

THE OPTIMIST

The fields were bleak and sodden.
    Not a wing
Or note enlivened the depressing wood;
A soiled and sullen, stubborn snowdrift stood
Beside the roadway. Winds came muttering
Of storms to be, and brought the chilly sting
    Of icebergs in their breath. Stalled cattle mooed
    Forth plaintive pleadings for the earth's green food.
No gleam, no hint of hope in anything.

The sky was blank and ashen, like the face
    Of some poor wretch who drains life's cup too fast
Yet, swaying to and fro, as if to fling
About chilled Nature its lithe arms of grace,
    Smiling with promise in the wintry blast,
The optimistic Willow spoke of spring.

THE PESSIMIST

The pessimistic locust, last to leaf,
Though all the world is glad, still talks of grief.

AN INSPIRATION

However the battle is ended,
　　Though proudly the victor comes
With fluttering flags and prancing nags
　　And echoing roll of drums,
Still truth proclaims this motto
　　In letters of living light,—
No question is ever settled
　　Until it is settled right.

Though the heel of the strong oppressor
　　May grind the weak in the dust;
And the voices of fame with one acclaim
　　May call him great and just,
Let those who applaud take warning.
　　And keep this motto in sight,—
No question is ever settled
　　Until it is settled right.

Let those who have failed take courage;
　　Though the enemy seems to have won,
Though his ranks are strong, if he be in the wrong
　　The battle is not yet done;

For, sure as the morning follows
        The darkest hour of the night,
No question is ever settled
        Until it is settled right.

O man bowed down with labour!
        O woman young, yet old!
O heart oppressed in the toiler's breast
        And crushed by the power of gold
Keep on with your weary battle
        Against triumphant might;
No question is ever settled
        Until it is settled right.

LIFE'S HARMONIES

Let no man pray that he know not sorrow,
 Let no soul ask to be free from pain,
For the gall of today is the sweet of tomorrow,
 And the moment's loss is the lifetime's gain.

Through want of a thing does its worth redouble,
 Through hunger's pangs does the feast content,
And only the heart that has harboured trouble
 Can fully rejoice when joy is sent.

Let no man shrink from the bitter tonics
 Of grief, and yearning, and need, and strife,
For the rarest chords in the soul's harmonics
 Are found in the minor strains of life.

PREPARATION

We must not force events, but rather make
The heart soil ready for their coming, as
The earth spreads carpets for the feet of Spring,
Or, with the strengthening tonic of the frost,
Prepares for winter. Should a July noon
Burst suddenly upon a frozen world
Small joy would follow, even though that world
Were longing for the Summer. Should the sting
Of sharp December pierce the heart of June,
What death and devastation would ensue!
All things are planned. The most majestic sphere
That whirls through space is governed and controlled
By supreme law, as is the blade of grass
Which through the bursting bosom of the earth
Creeps up to kiss the light. Poor, puny man
Alone doth strive and battle with the Force
Which rules all lives and worlds, and he alone
Demands effect before producing cause.
How vain the hope! We cannot harvest joy
Until we sow the seed, and God alone
Knows when that seed has ripened. Oft we stand
And watch the ground with anxious, brooding eyes,
Complaining of the slow, unfruitful yield,
Not knowing that the shadow of ourselves
Keeps off the sunlight and delays result.

Sometimes our fierce impatience of desire
Doth like a sultry May force tender shoots
Of half-formed pleasures and unshaped events
To ripen prematurely, and we reap
But disappointment; or we rot the germs
With briny tears ere they have time to grow.
While stars are born and mighty planets die
And hissing comets scorch the brow of space,
The Universe keeps its eternal calm.
Through patient preparation, year on year,
The earth endures the travail of the Spring
And Winter's desolation. So our souls
In grand submission to a higher law
Should move serene through all the ills of life
Believing them masked joys.

GETHSEMANE

In golden youth when seems the earth
A Summer-land of singing mirth,
When souls are glad and hearts are light,
And not a shadow lurks in sight,
We do not know it, but there lieu
Somewhere veiled under evening skies
A garden which we all must see—
The garden of Gethsemane.

With joyous steps we go our ways,
Love lends a halo to our days;
Light sorrows sail like clouds afar,
We laugh, and say how strong we are.
We hurry on; and hurrying, go
Close to the borderland of woe
That waits for you, and waits for me—
Forever waits Gethsemane.

Down shadowy lanes, across strange streams,
Bridged over by our broken dreams;
Behind the misty caps of years,
Beyond the great salt fount of tears,

The garden lies. Strive as you may,
You cannot miss it in your way;
All paths that have been, or shall be,
Pass somewhere through Gethsemane.

All those who journey, soon or late,
Must pass within the garden's gate;
Must kneel alone in darkness there,
And battle with some fierce despair.
God pity those who cannot say,
"Not mine but Thine"; who only pray
"Let this cup pass," and cannot see
The *purpose* in Gethsemane.

GOD'S MEASURE

God measures souls by their capacity
For entertaining his best Angel, Love.
Who loveth most is nearest kin to God,
Who is all Love, or Nothing.

     He who sits
And looks out on the palpitating world,
And feels his heart swell in him large enough
To hold all men within it, he is near
His great Creator's standard, though he dwells
Outside the pale of churches, and knows not
A feast-day from a fast-day, or a line
Of Scripture even. What God wants of us
Is that outreaching bigness that ignores
All littleness of aims, or loves, or creeds,
And clasps all Earth and Heaven in its embrace.

NOBLESSE OBLIGE

I hold it the duty of one who is gifted
    And specially dowered in all men's sight,
To know no rest till his life is lifted
    Fully up to his great gifts' height.

He must mould the man into rare completeness,
    For gems are set only in gold refined.
He must fashion his thoughts into perfect sweetness.
    And cast out folly and pride from his mind.

For he who drinks from a god's gold fountain
    Of art or music or rhythmic song
Must sift from his soul the chaff of malice,
    And weed from his heart the roots of wrong.

Great gifts should be worn, like a crown befitting,
    And not like gems in a beggar's hands!
And the toil must be constant and unremitting
    Which lifts up the king to the crown's demands.

THROUGH TEARS

An artist toiled over his pictures;
    He laboured by night and by day,
He struggled for glory and honour
    But the world, it had nothing to say.
His walls were ablaze with the splendours
    We see in the beautiful skies;
But the world beheld only the colours
    That were made out of chemical dyes.

Time sped. And he lived, loved, and suffered;
    He passed through the valley of grief.
Again he toiled over his canvas,
    Since in labour alone was relief.
It showed not the splendour of colours
    Of those of his earlier years;
But the world? the world bowed down before it
    Because it was painted with tears.

A poet was gifted with genius,
    And he sang, and he sang all the days.
He wrote for the praise of the people,
    But the people accorded no praise.

Oh! his songs were as blithe as the morning,
　　As sweet as the music of birds;
But the world had no homage to offer,
　　Because they were nothing but words.

Time sped. And the poet through sorrow
　　Became like his suffering kind.
Again he toiled over his poems
　　To lighten the grief of his mind.
They were not so flowing and rhythmic
　　As those of his earlier years;
But the world? lo! it offered its homage,
　　Because they were written in tears.

So ever the price must be given
　　By those seeking glory in art;
So ever the world is repaying
　　The grief-stricken, suffering heart.
The happy must ever be humble;
　　Ambition must wait for the years
Ere hoping to win the approval
　　Of a world that looks on through its tears.

WHAT WE NEED

What does our country need? No armies standing
  With sabres gleaming ready for the fight;
Not increased navies, skilful and commanding,
  To bound the waters with an iron might;
Not haughty men with glutted purses trying
  To purchase souls, and keep the power of place;
Not jewelled dolls with one another vying
  For palms of beauty, elegance, and grace.

But we want women, strong of soul, yet lowly,
  With that rare meekness, born of gentleness;
Women whose lives are pure and clean and holy,
  The women whom all little children bless;
Brave, earnest women, helpful to each other,
  With finest scorn for all things low and mean;
Women who hold the names of wife and mother
  Far nobler than the title of a queen.

Oh! these are they who mould the men of story,
  These mothers, ofttimes shorn of grace and youth,
Who, worn and weary, ask no greater glory
  Than making some young soul the home of truth;

Who sow in hearts all fallow for the sowing
    The seeds of virtue and of scorn for sin,
And, patient, watch the beauteous harvest growing
    And weed out tares which crafty hands cast in;

Women who do not hold the gift of beauty
    As some rare treasure to be bought and sold.
But guard it as a precious aid to duty—
    The outer framing of the inner gold;
Women who, low above their cradles bending,
    Let flattery's voice go by, and give no heed,
While their pure prayers like incense are ascending
    These are our country's pride, our country's need,

PLEA TO SCIENCE

O Science, reaching backward through the distance,
    Most earnest child of God,
Exposing all the secrets of existence,
    With thy divining rod,
I bid thee speed up to the heights supernal,
    Clear thinker, ne'er sufficed;
Go seek and bind the laws and truths eternal,
    But leave me Christ.

Upon the vanity of pious sages
    Let in the light of day;
Break down the superstitions of all ages—
    Thrust bigotry away;
Stride on, and bid all stubborn foes defiance,
    Let Truth and Reason reign:
But I beseech thee, O Immortal Science,
    Let Christ remain.

What canst thou give to help me bear my crosses,
    In place of Him, my Lord?
And what to recompense for all my losses,
    And bring me sweet reward?

Thou couldst not with thy clear, cold eyes of reason,
    Thou couldst not comfort me
Like One who passed through that tear-blotted season
    In sad Gethsemane!

Through all the weary, wearing hour of sorrow,
    What word that thou hast said
Would make me strong to wait for some tomorrow
    When I should find my dead?
When I am weak, and desolate, and lonely—
    And prone to follow wrong?
Not thou, O Science—Christ, my Saviour, only
    Can make me strong.

Thou art so cold, so lofty, and so distant,
    Though great my need might be,
No prayer, however constant and persistent,
    Could bring thee down to me.
Christ stands so near, to help me through each hour,
    To guide me day by day
O Science, sweeping all before thy power—
    Leave Christ, I pray!

RESPITE

The mighty conflict, which we call existence,
   Doth wear upon the body and the soul,
Our vital forces wasted in resistance,
   So much there is to conquer and control.

The rock which meets the billows with defiance,
   Undaunted and unshaken day by day,
In spite of its unyielding self-reliance,
   Is by the warfare surely worn away.

And there are depths and heights of strong emotions
   That surge at times within the human breast,
More fierce than all the tides of all the oceans
   Which sweep on ever in divine unrest.

I sometimes think the rock worn with adventures,
   And sad with thoughts of conflicts yet to be,
Must envy the frail reed which no one censures,
   When, overcome, 'tis swallowed by the sea.

This life is all resistance and repression.
   Dear God, if in that other world unseen,
Not rest we find, but new life and progression,
   Grant us a respite in the grave between.

SONG

O praise me not with your lips, dear one!
    Though your tender words I prize.
But dearer by far is the soulful gaze
    Of your eyes, your beautiful eyes
    Your tender, loving eyes.

O chide me not with your lips, dear one!
    Though I cause your bosom sighs.
You can make repentance deeper far
    By your sad, reproving eyes,
    Your sorrowful, troubled eyes.

Words, at the best, are but hollow sounds;
    Above, in the beaming skies,
The constant stars say never a word,
    But only smile with their eyes—
    Smile on with their lustrous eyes.

Then breathe no vow with your lips, dear one;
    On the winged wind speech flies.
But I read the truth of your noble heart
    In your soulful, speaking eyes—
    In your deep and beautiful eyes.

MY SHIPS

If all the ships I have at sea
Should come a-sailing home to me,
Ah, well! the harbour could not hold
So many sails as there would be
If all my ships came in from sea.

If half my ships came home from sea,
And brought their precious freight to me,
Ah, well! I should have wealth as great
As any king who sits in state—
So rich the treasures that would be
In half my ships now out at sea.

If just one ship I have at sea
Should come a-sailing home to me,
Ah, well! the storm-clouds then might frown
For if the others all went down,
Still rich and proud and glad I'd be
If that one ship came back to me.

If that one ship went down at sea,
And all the others came to me,
Weighed down with gems and wealth untold,
With glory, honours, riches, gold,
The poorest soul on earth I'd be
If that one ship came not to me.

O skies, be calm! O winds, blow free—
Blow all my ships safe home to me!
But if thou sendest some a-wrack,
To never more come sailing back,
Send any—all that skim the sea,
But bring my love-ship home to me.

HER LOVE

The sands upon the ocean side
That change about with every tide,
And never true to one abide,
    A woman's love I liken to.

The summer zephyrs, light and vain,
That sing the same alluring strain
To every grass blade on the plain—
    A woman's love is nothing more.

The sunshine of an April day
That comes to warm you with its ray,
But while you smile has flown away—
    A woman's love is like to this.

God made poor woman with no heart,
But gave her skill, and tact, and art,
And so she lives, and plays her part.
    We must not blame, but pity her.

She leans to man—but just to hear
The praise he whispers in her ear;
Herself, not him, she holdeth dear—
    O fool! to be deceived by her.

To sate her selfish thirst she quaffs
The love of strong hearts in sweet draughts,
Then throws them lightly by and laughs,
    Too weak to understand their pain.

As changeful as the winds that blow
From every region to and fro,
Devoid of heart, she cannot know
    The suffering of a human heart.

IF

Dear love, if you and I could sail away,
    With snowy pennons to the winds unfurled,
Across the waters of some unknown bay,
    And find some island far from all the world;

If we could dwell there, evermore alone,
    While unrecorded years slip by apace,
Forgetting and forgotten and unknown
    By aught save native song-birds of the place;

If Winter never visited that land,
    And Summer's lap spilled o'er with fruits and flowers,
And tropic trees cast shade on every hand,
    And twinèd boughs formed sleep-inviting bowers;

If from the fashions of the world set free,
    And hid away from all its jealous strife,
I lived alone for you, and you for me—
    Ah! then, dear love, how sweet were wedded life.

But since we dwell here in the crowded way,
    Where hurrying throngs rush by to seek for gold,
And all is commonplace and work-a-day
    As soon as love's young honeymoon grows old;

Since fashion rules and nature yields to art,
    And life is hurt by daily jar and fret,
'Tis best to shut such dreams down in the heart
    And go our ways alone, love, and forget.

LOVE'S BURIAL

Let us clear a little space,
And make Love a burial-place.

He is dead, dear, as you see,
And he wearies you and me.

Growing heavier, day by day,
Let us bury him, I say.

Wings of dead white butterflies,
These shall shroud him, as he lies

In his casket rich and rare,
Made of finest maiden-hair.

With the pollen of the rose
Let us his white eyelids close.

Put the rose thorn in his hand,
Shorn of leaves—you understand.

Let some holy water fall
On his dead face, tears of gall—

As we kneel to him and say,
"Dreams to dreams," and turn away.

Those gravediggers, Doubt, Distrust,
They will lower him to the dust.

Let us part here with a kiss—
You go that way, I go this.

Since we buried Love today
We will walk a separate way.

"LOVE IS ENOUGH"

Love is enough. Let us not ask for gold.
    Wealth breeds false aims, and pride, and selfishness;
In those serene, Arcadian days of old
    Men gave no thought to princely homes and dress.
The gods who dwelt on fair Olympia's height
Lived only for dear love and love's delight.
    Love is enough.

Love is enough. Why should we care for fame?
    Ambition is a most unpleasant guest:
It lures us with the glory of a name
    Far from the happy haunts of peace and rest.
Let us stay here in this secluded place
Made beautiful by love's endearing grace!
    Love is enough.

Love is enough. Why should we strive for power?
    It brings men only envy and distrust.
The poor world's homage pleases but an hour,
    And earthly honours vanish in the dust.
The grandest lives are ofttimes desolate;
Let me be loved, and let who will be great.
    Love is enough.

Love is enough. Why should we ask for more?
   What greater gift have gods vouchsafed to men?
What better boon of all their precious store
   Than our fond hearts that love and love again?
Old love may die; new love is just as sweet;
And life is fair and all the world complete:
   Love is enough!

LIFE IS A PRIVILEGE

Life is a privilege. Its youthful days
Shine with the radiance of continuous Mays.
To live, to breathe, to wonder and desire,
To feed with dreams the heart's perpetual fire,
To thrill with virtuous passions, and to glow
With great ambitions—in one hour to know
The depths and heights of feeling—God! in truth,
How beautiful, how beautiful is youth!

Life is a privilege. Like some rare rose
The mysteries of the human mind unclose.
What marvels lie in earth, and air, and sea!
What stores of knowledge wait our opening key!
What sunny roads of happiness lead out
Beyond the realms of indolence and doubt!
And what large pleasures smile upon and bless
The busy avenues of usefulness!

Life is a privilege. Though noontide fades
And shadows fall along the winding glades,
Though joy-blooms wither in the autumn air,
Yet the sweet scent of sympathy is there.

Pale sorrow leads us closer to our kind,
And in the serious hours of life we find
Depths in the souls of men which lend new worth
And majesty to this brief span of earth.

Life is a privilege. If some sad fate
Sends us alone to seek the exit gate,
If men forsake us and as shadows fall,
Still does the supreme privilege of all
Come in that reaching upward of the soul
To find the welcoming Presence at the goal,
And in the Knowledge that our feet have trod
Paths that led from, and must wind back, to God.

INSIGHT

Sirs, when you pity us, I say
You waste your pity. Let it stay,
Well corked and stored upon your shelves,
Until you need it for yourselves.

We do appreciate God's thought
In forming you, before He brought
Us into life. His art was crude,
But oh! so virile in its rude,

Large, elemental strength; and then
He learned His trade in making men,
Learned how to mix and mould the clay
And fashion in a finer way.

How fine that skilful way can be
You need but lift your eyes to see;
And we are glad God placed you there
To lift your eyes and find us fair.

Apprentice labour though you were,
He made you great enough to stir
The best and deepest depths of us,
And we are glad He made you thus.

Aye! we are glad of many things;
God strung our hearts with such fine strings
The least breath moves them, and we hear
Music where silence greets your ear.

We suffer so? But women's souls,
Like violet-powder dropped on coals,
Give forth their best in anguish. Oh
The subtle secrets that we know

Of joy in sorrow, strange delights
Of ecstasy in pain-filled nights,
And mysteries of gain in loss
Known but to Christ upon the cross!

Our tears are pitiful to you?
Look how the heaven-reflecting dew
Dissolves its life in tears. The sand
Meanwhile lies hard upon the strand.

How could your pity find a place
For us, the mothers of the race?
Men may be fathers unaware,
So poor the title is you wear.

But mothers—who that crown adorns
Knows all its mingled blooms and thorns,
And she whose feet that pain hath trod
Hath walked upon the heights with God.

No, offer us not pity's cup.
There is no looking down or up
Between us; eye looks straight in eye:
Born equals, so we live and die.

A WOMAN'S ANSWER

You call me an angel of love and of light,
    A being of goodness and heavenly fire,
Sent out from God's kingdom to guide you aright,
    In paths where your spirit may mount and aspire,
You say that I glow like a star on its course,
Like a ray from the altar, a spark from the source.

Now list to my answer—let all the world hear it,
    I speak unafraid what I know to be true—
A pure, faithful love is the creative spirit
    Which make women angels! I live but in you.
We are bound soul to soul by life's holiest laws;
If I am an angel—why, you are the cause.

As my ship skims the sea, I look up from the deck.
    Fair, firm at the wheel shines Love's beautiful form.
And shall I curse the bark that last night went to wreck
    By the pilot abandoned to darkness and storm?
My craft is no stauncher, she too had been lost
Had the wheelman deserted, or slept at his post.

I laid down the wealth of my soul at your feet
    (Some woman does this for some man every day).
No desperate creature who walks in the street
    Has a wickeder heart than I might have, I say,
Had you wantonly misused the treasures you won—
As so many men with heart-riches have done.

This fire from God's altar, this holy love-flame,
    That burns like sweet incense forever for you,
Might now be a wild conflagration of shame,
    Had you tortured my heart, or been base or untrue.
For angels and devils are cast in one mould,
Till love guides them upward or downward, I hold.

I tell you the women who make fervent wives
    And sweet tender mothers, had Fate been less fair,
Are the women who might have abandoned their lives
    To the madness that springs from and ends in despair.
As the fire on the hearth which sheds brightness around,
Neglected, may level the walls to the ground.

The world makes grave errors in judging these things.
    Great good and great evil are born in one breast:
Love horns us and hoofs us, or gives us our wings,
    And the best could be worst, as the worst could be best.
You must thank your own worth for what I grew to be,
For the demon lurked under the angel in me.

THE WORLD'S NEED

So many gods, so many creeds,
    So many paths that wind and wind,
    While just the art of being kind,
Is all the sad world needs.

"REJOICE, AND MEN WILL SEEK YOU"

POEMS OF PASSION

Oh, you who read some song that I have sung,
What know you of the soul from whence it sprung?

Dost dream the poet ever speaks aloud
His secret thought unto the listening crowd?

Go take the murmuring sea-shell from the shore:
You have its shape, its color and no more.

It tells not one of those vast mysteries
That lie beneath the surface of the seas.

Our songs are shells, cast out by-waves of thought;
Here, take them at your pleasure; but think not

You've seen beneath the surface of the waves,
Where lie our shipwrecks and our coral caves.

THE POET'S SONG

PREFACE

Among the twelve hundred poems which have emanated from my too prolific pen there are some forty or fifty which treat entirely of that emotion which has been denominated "the grand passion"—love. A few of those are of an extremely fiery character.

When I issued my collection known as "Maurine, and Other Poems," I purposely omitted all save two or three of these. I had been frequently accused of writing only sentimental verses; and I took pleasure and pride in presenting to the public a volume which contained more than one hundred poems upon other than sentimental topics. But no sooner was the book published than letters of regret came to me from friends and strangers, and from all quarters of the globe, asking why this or that love poem had been omitted. These regrets were repeated to me by so many people that I decided to collect and issue these poems in a small volume to be called "Poems of Passion." By the word "Passion" I meant the "grand passion" of love. To those who take exception to the title of the book I would suggest an early reference to Webster's definitions of the word.

Since this volume has caused so much agitation throughout the entire country, and even sent a tremor across the Atlantic into the Old World, I beg leave to make a few statements concerning some of the poems.

The excitement of mingled horror and amaze seems to center upon four poems, namely: "Delilah," "Ad Finem," "Conversion," and "Communism."

"Delilah" was written and first published in 1877. I had been reading history, and became stirred by the power of such women as Aspasia and Cleopatra over such grand men as Antony, Socrates, and Pericles. Under the influence of this feeling I dashed off "Delilah," which I meant to be an expression of the powerful fascination of such a woman upon the memory of a man, even as he neared the hour of death. If the poem is immoral, then the history which inspired it is immoral. I consider it my finest effort.

"Ad Finem" was written in 1878. I think there are few women of strong character and affections who cannot, from either experience or observation, understand the violent intensity of regret and despair which sometimes takes possession of the human heart after the loss by death, fate, or the force of circumstances, of some one very dear.

In "Ad Finem" I intended to give voice to this very common experience of almost every heart. Many noble women have since told me that the poem was true to life. It is not, as many people have wilfully or stupidly construed it, a bit of poetical advice to womankind to "barter the joys of Paradise" for "just one kiss." It is simply an illustration of a moment of turbulent anguish and vehement despair, such moments of unreasoning and overwhelming sorrow as the most moral people may experience during a lifetime.

In "Communism" I endeavored to use a new simile in illustrating that somewhat hackneyed theme of the supremacy of Love over Reason; and simply to carry out my idea I represented the violent uprising of the Communist emotions against King Reason.

"Conversion" was suggested to me by the remark of a gentleman friend. In speaking to me of the woman he loved, he said: "I have always been a skeptic regarding the existence of heaven, but I am so much happier in my love for this woman than I ever supposed it possible for me to be on earth that I begin to believe that the tales of heavenly raptures may be true."

I embodied his idea in the poem which has brought, with a few others, so much censure and criticism upon this volume, although it contains nearly seventy-five other selections quite irreproachable in character, however faulty they may be in construction.

It is impossible to pursue a successful literary career and follow the advice of all one's "best friends." I have received severe censure from my orthodox friends for writing liberal verses. My liberal friends condemn my devout and religious poems as "aiding superstition." My early temperance verses were pronounced "fanatical trash" by others.

With all due thanks and appreciation for the kind motives which interest so many dear friends in my career, I yet feel compelled to follow the light which my own intellect and judgment cast upon my way, rather than any one of the many conflicting rays which other minds would lend me.

ELLA WHEELER.

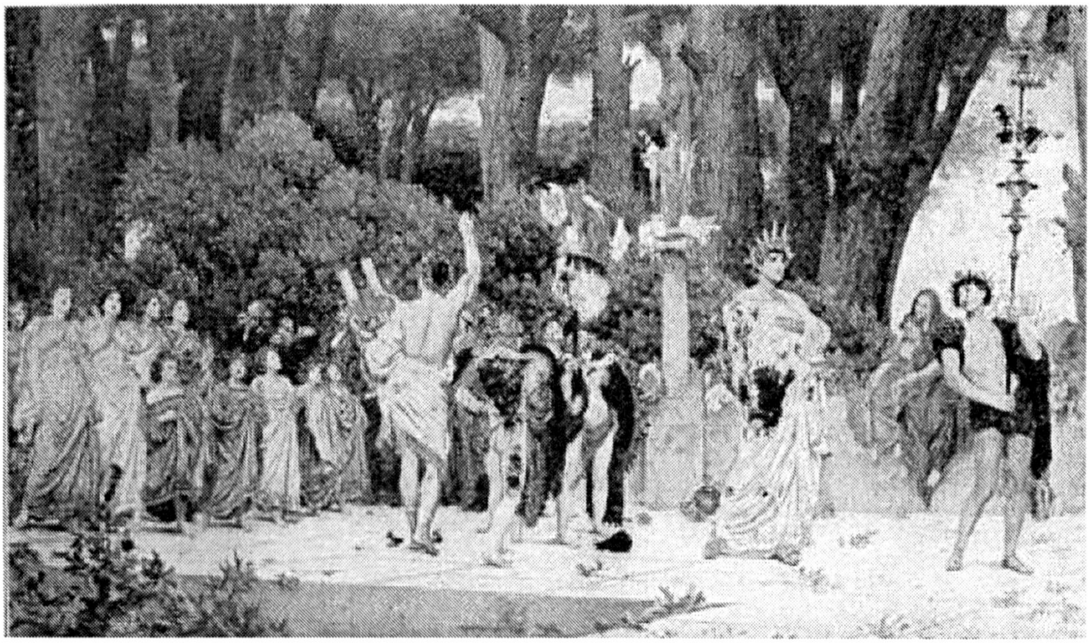

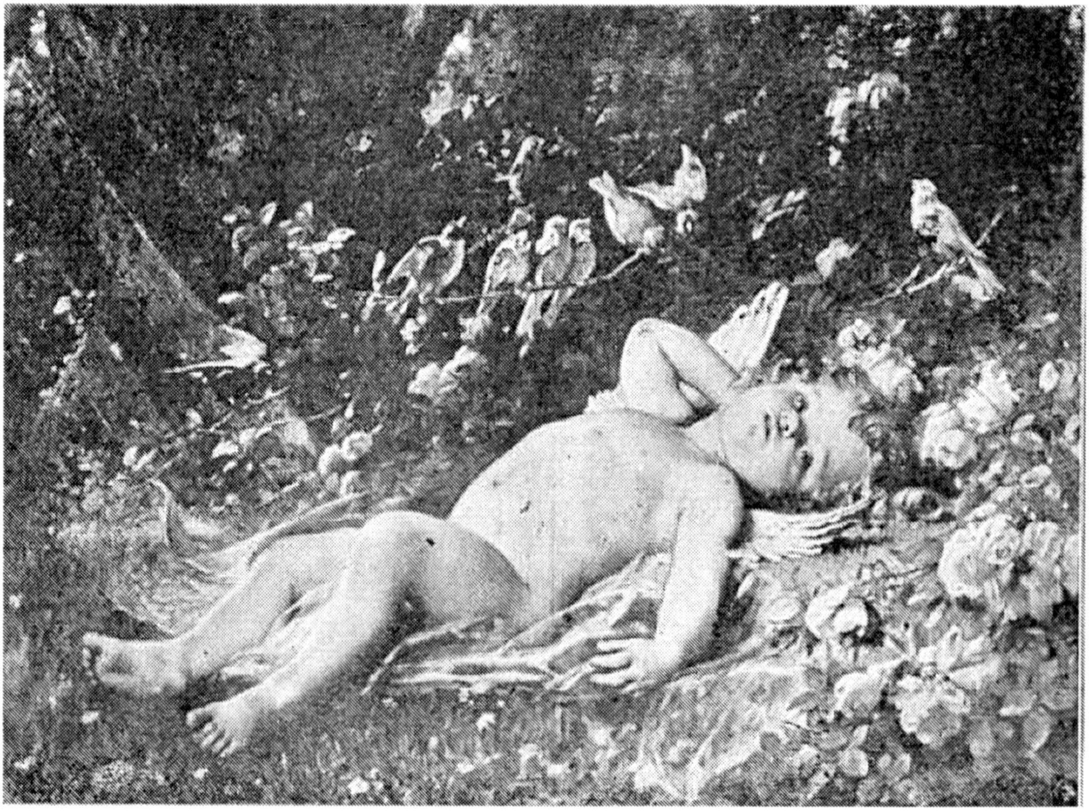

LOVE'S LANGUAGE.

How does Love speak?
In the faint flush upon the tell-tale cheek,
And in the pallor that succeeds it; by
The quivering lid of an averted eye—
The smile that proves the patent to a sigh—
Thus doth Love speak.

How does Love speak?
By the uneven heart-throbs, and the freak
Of bounding pulses that stand still and ache,
While new emotions, like strange barges, make
Along vein-channels their disturbing course;
Still as the dawn, and with the dawn's swift force—
Thus doth Love speak.

How does Love speak?
In the avoidance of that which we seek—
The sudden silence and reserve when near—
The eye that glistens with an unshed tear—
The joy that seems the counterpart of fear,
As the alarmed heart leaps in the breast,
And knows and names and greets its godlike guest—
Thus doth Love speak.

How does Love speak?
In the proud spirit suddenly grown meek—
The haughty heart grown humble; in the tender
And unnamed light that floods the world with splendor;
In the resemblance which the fond eyes trace
In all fair things to one beloved face;
In the shy touch of hands that thrill and tremble;
In looks and lips that can no more dissemble—
          Thus doth Love speak.

How does Love speak?
In the wild words that uttered seem so weak
They shrink ashamed to silence; in the fire
Glance strikes with glance, swift flashing high and higher
Like lightnings that precede the mighty storm;
In the deep, soulful stillness; in the warm,
Impassioned tide that sweeps through throbbing veins
Between the shores of keen delight and pains;
In the embrace where madness melts in bliss,
And in the convulsive rapture of a kiss—
          Thus doth Love speak.

LOVE'S LANGUAGE

IMPATIENCE.

How can I wait until you come to me?
    The once fleet mornings linger by the way,
Their sunny smiles touched with malicious glee
    At my unrest; they seem to pause, and play
    Like truant children, while I sigh and say,
        How can I wait?

How can I wait? Of old, the rapid hours
        Refused to pause or loiter with me long;
But now they idly fill their hands with flowers,
    And make no haste, but slowly stroll among
    The summer blooms, not heeding my one song,
        How can I wait?

How can I wait? The nights alone are kind;
    They reach forth to a future day, and bring
Sweet dreams of you to people all my mind;
    And time speeds by on light and airy wing.
    I feast upon your face, I no more sing,
        How can I wait?

How can I wait? The morning breaks the spell
    A pitying night has flung upon my soul.
You are not near me, and I know full well
    My heart has need of patience and control;
    Before we meet, hours, days, and weeks must roll.
            How can I wait?

How can I wait? Oh, love, how can I wait
    Until the sunlight of your eyes shall shine
Upon my world that seems so desolate?
    Until your hand-clasp warms my blood like wine;
    Until you come again, oh, love of mine,
            How can I wait?

COMMUNISM.

When my blood flows calm as a purling river,
    When my heart is asleep and my brain has sway,
It is then that I vow we must part forever,
    That I will forget you, and put you away
Out of my life, as a dream is banished
    Out of the mind when the dreamer awakes;
That I know it will be, when the spell has vanished,
    Better for both of our sakes.

When the court of the mind is ruled by Reason,
    I know it is wiser for us to part;
But Love is a spy who is plotting treason,
    In league with that warm, red rebel, the Heart.
They whisper to me that the King is cruel,
    That his reign is wicked, his law a sin;
And every word they utter is fuel
    To the flame that smoulders within.

And on nights like this, when my blood runs riot
    With the fever of youth and its mad desires,
When my brain in vain bids my heart be quiet,
    When my breast seems the centre of lava-fires,
Oh, then is the time when most I miss you,
    And I swear by the stars and my soul and say
That I will have you and hold you and kiss you,
    Though the whole world stands in the way.

And like Communists, as mad, as disloyal,
    My fierce emotions roam out of their lair;
They hate King Reason for being royal;
    They would fire his castle, and burn him there.
Oh, Love! they would clasp you and crush you and kill you,
    In the insurrection of uncontrol.
Across the miles, does this wild war thrill you
    That is raging in my soul?

"LOVE'S IMPATIENCE"

THE COMMON LOT.

It is a common fate—a woman's lot—
    To waste on one the riches of her soul,
Who takes the wealth she gives him, but cannot
    Repay the interest, and much less the whole.

As I look up into your eyes and wait
    For some response to my fond gaze and touch,
It seems to me there is no sadder fate
    Than to be doomed to loving overmuch.

Are you not kind? Ah, yes, so very kind—
    So thoughtful of my comfort, and so true.
Yes, yes, dear heart; but I, not being blind,
    Know that I am not loved as I love you.

One tenderer word, a little longer kiss,
    Will fill my soul with music and with song;
And if you seem abstracted, or I miss
    The heart-tone from your voice, my world goes wrong.

And oftentimes you think me childish—weak—
    When at some thoughtless word the tears will start;
You cannot understand how aught you speak
    Has power to stir the depths of my poor heart.

I cannot help it, dear,—I wish I could,
    Or feign indifference where I now adore;
For if I seemed to love you less you would,
    Manlike, I have no doubt, love me the more.

'Tis a sad gift, that much applauded thing,
    A constant heart; for fact doth daily prove
That constancy finds oft a cruel sting,
    While fickle natures win the deeper love.

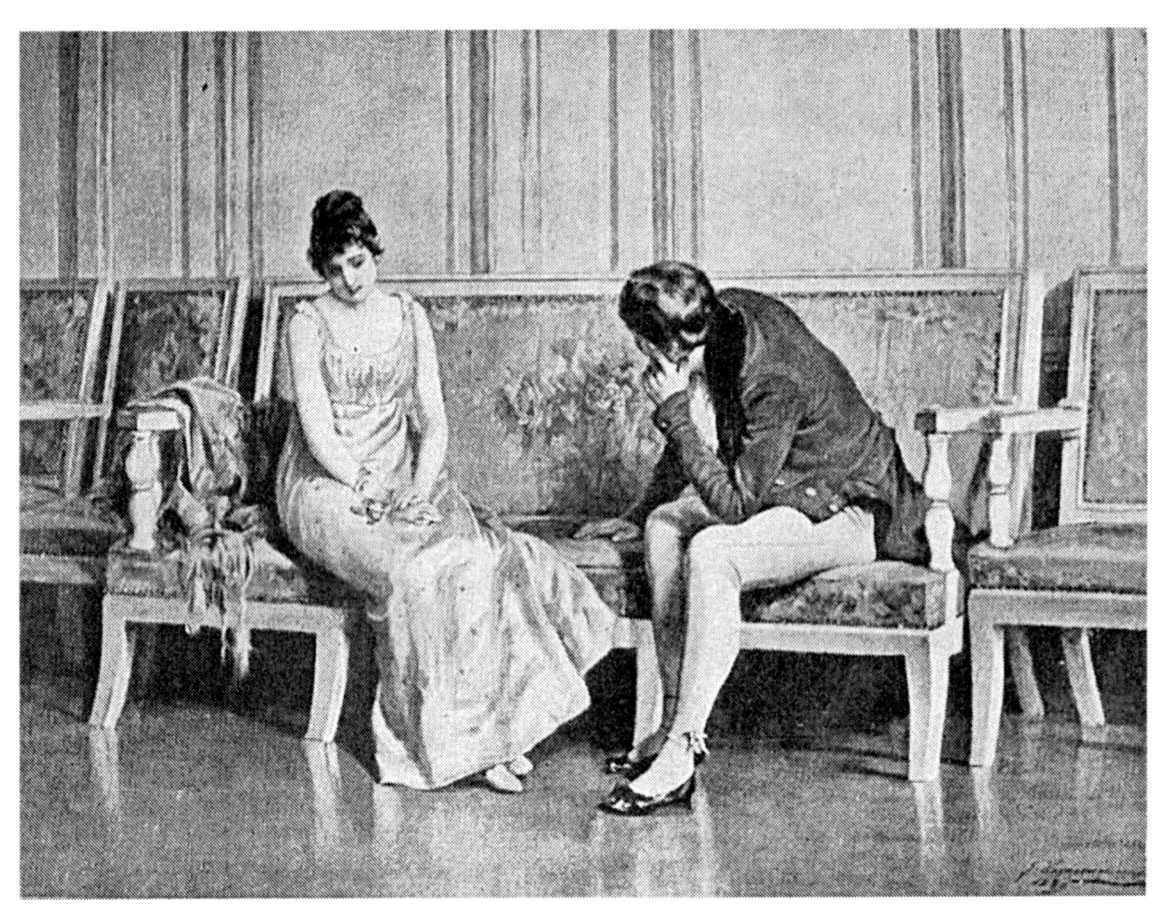

COMMON LOT

INDIVIDUALITY.

O yes, I love you, and with all my heart;
    Just as a weaker woman loves her own,
Better than I love my beloved art,
    Which, till you came, reigned royally, alone,
My king, my master. Since I saw your face
I have dethroned it, and you hold that place.

I am as weak as other women are:
    Your frown can make the whole world like a tomb;
Your smile shines brighter than the sun, by far.
    Sometimes I think there is not space or room
In all the earth for such a love as mine,
And it soars up to breathe in realms divine.

I know that your desertion or neglect
    Could break my heart, as women's hearts do break.
If my wan days had nothing to expect
    From your love's splendor, all joy would forsake
The chambers of my soul. Yes, this is true.
And yet, and yet—one thing I keep from you.

There is a subtle part of me, which went
    Into my long pursued and worshipped art;
Though your great love fills me with such content
    No other love finds room now, in my heart.

Yet that rare essence was my art's alone.
Thank God, you cannot grasp it; 'tis mine own.

Thank God, I say, for while I love you so,
With that vast love, as passionate as tender,
I feel an exultation as I know
I have not made you a complete surrender.
Here is my body; bruise it, if you will,
And break my heart; I have that *something* still.

You cannot grasp it. Seize the breath of morn
    Or bind the perfume of the rose, as well.
God put it in my soul when I was born;
    It is not mine to give away, or sell,
Or offer up on any altar shrine.
It was my art's; and when not art's, 'tis mine,

For love's sake I can put the art away,
    Or anything which stands 'twixt me and you.
But that strange essence God bestowed, I say,
    To permeate the work He gave to do:
And it cannot be drained, dissolved, or sent
Through any channel save the one He meant.

FRIENDSHIP AFTER LOVE.

After the fierce midsummer all ablaze
       Has burned itself to ashes, and expires
       In the intensity of its own fires,
There come the mellow, mild, St. Martin days,
Crowned with the calm of peace, but sad with haze.
       So after Love has led us, till he tires
       Of his own throes and torments and desires,
Comes large-eyed friendship: with a restful gaze
He beckons us to follow, and across
       Cool, verdant vales we wander free from care.
       Is it a touch of frost lies in the air?
Why are we haunted with a sense of loss?
       We do not wish the pain back, or the heat;
       And yet, and yet, these days are incomplete.

LOVE TRIUMPANT

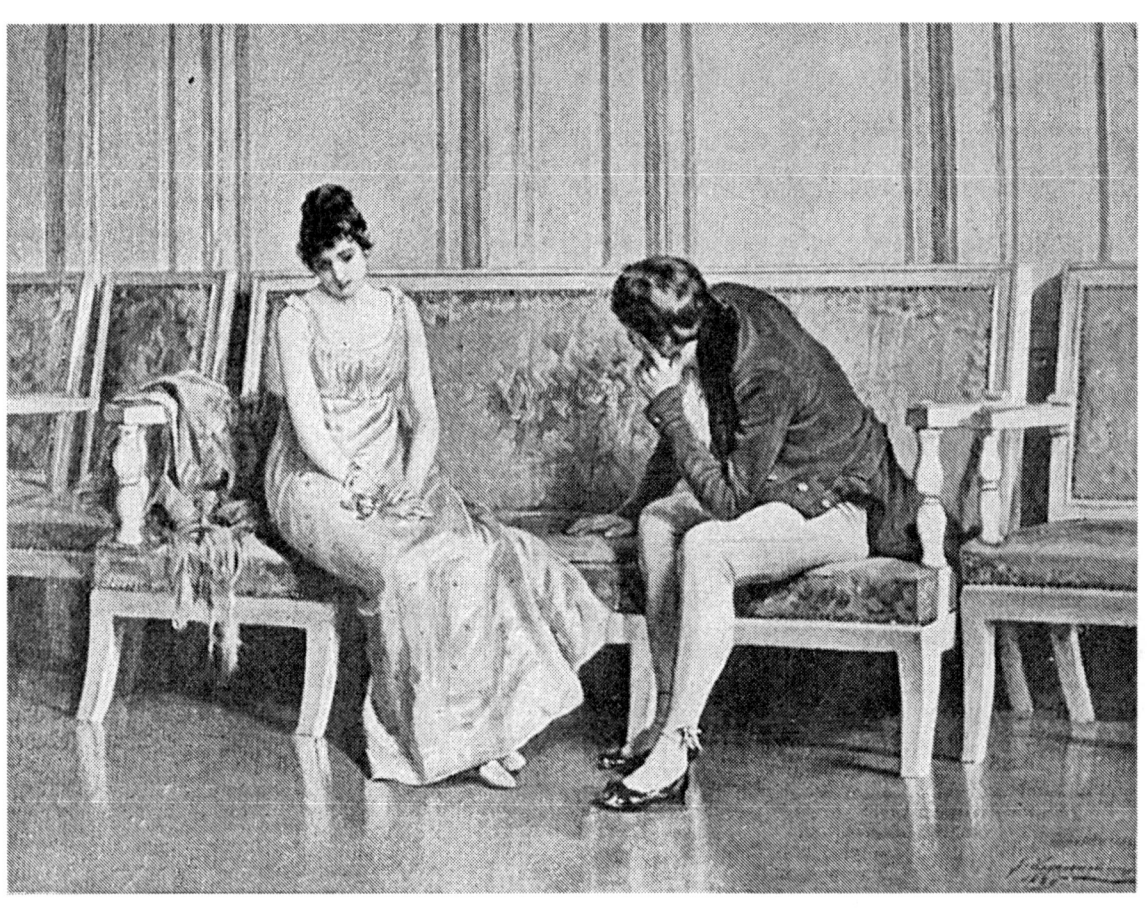

QUERIES.

Well, how has it been with you since we met
    That last strange time of a hundred times?
When we met to swear that we could forget—
    I your caresses, and you my rhymes—
The rhyme of my lays that rang like a bell,
And the rhyme of my heart with yours, as well?

How has it been since we drank that last kiss,
    That was bitter with lees of the wasted wine,
When the tattered remains of a threadbare bliss,
    And the worn-out shreds of a joy divine,
With a year's best dreams and hopes, were cast
Into the rag-bag of the Past?

Since Time, the rag-buyer, hurried away,
    With a chuckle of glee at a bargain made,
Did you discover, like me, one day,
    That, hid in the folds of those garments frayed,
Were priceless jewels and diadems—
The soul's best treasures, the heart's best gems?

Have you, too, found that you could not supply
	The place of those jewels so rare and chaste?
Do all that you borrow or beg or buy
	Prove to be nothing but skilful paste?
Have you found pleasure, as I found art,
Not all-sufficient to fill your heart?

Do you sometimes sigh for the tattered shreds
	Of the old delight that we cast away,
And find no worth in the silken threads
	Of newer fabrics we wear today?
Have you thought the bitter of that last kiss
Better than sweets of a later bliss?

What idle queries!—or yes or no—
	Whatever your answer, I understand
That there is no pathway by which we can go
	Back to the dead past's wonderland;
And the gems he purchased from me, from you,
There is no rebuying from Time, the Jew.

"THE OLD DELIGHT THAT WE CAST AWAY"

UPON THE SAND.

All love that has not friendship for its base
    Is like a mansion built upon the sand.
    Though brave its walls as any in the land,
And its tall turrets lift their heads in grace;
Though skilful and accomplished artists trace
    Most beautiful designs on every hand,
    And gleaming statues in dim niches stand,
And fountains play in some flow'r-hidden place:

Yet, when from the frowning east a sudden gust
    Of adverse fate is blown, or sad rains fall,
    Day in, day out, against its yielding wall,
Lo! the fair structure crumbles to the dust.
    Love, to endure life's sorrow and earth's woe,
    Needs friendship's solid mason-work below.

REUNITED.

Let us begin, dear love, where we left off;
    Tie up the broken threads of that old dream,
    And go on happy as before, and seem
Lovers again, though all the world may scoff.

Let us forget the graves which lie between
    Our parting and our meeting, and the tears
    That rusted out the gold-work of the years,
The frosts that fell upon our gardens green.

Let us forget the cold, malicious Fate
    Who made our loving hearts her idle toys,
    And once more revel in the old sweet joys
Of happy love. Nay, it is not too late!

Forget the deep-ploughed furrows in my brow;
    Forget the silver gleaming in my hair;
    Look only in my eyes! Oh! darling, there
The old love shone no warmer then than now.

Down in the tender deeps of thy dear eyes
    I find the lost sweet memory of my youth,
    Bright with the holy radiance of thy truth,
And hallowed with the blue of summer skies.

Tie up the broken threads and let us go,
    Like reunited lovers, hand in hand,
    Back, and yet onward, to the sunny land
Of our To Be, which was our Long Ago.

WHAT SHALL WE DO?

Here now forevermore our lives must part.
    My path leads there, and yours another way.
What shall we do with this fond love, dear heart?
    It grows a heavier burden day by day.

Hide it? In all earth's caverns, void and vast,
    There is not room enough to hide it, dear;
Not even the mighty storehouse of the past
    Could cover it from our own eyes, I fear.

Drown it? Why, were the contents of each ocean
    Merged into one great sea, too shallow then
Would be its waters to sink this emotion
    So deep it could not rise to life again.

Burn it? In all the furnace flames below,
    It would not in a thousand years expire.
Nay! it would thrive, exult, expand, and grow,
    For from its very birth it fed on fire.

Starve it? Yes, yes, that is the only way.
    Give it no food, of glance, or word, or sigh;
No memories, even, of any bygone day;
    No crumbs of vain regrets—so let it die.

"THE BEAUTIFUL BLUE DANUBE."

They drift down the hall together;
    He smiles in her lifted eyes;
Like waves of that mighty river,
    The strains of the "Danube" rise.
They float on its rhythmic measure
    Like leaves on a summer-stream;
And here, in this scene of pleasure,
    I bury my sweet, dead dream.

Through the cloud of her dusky tresses,
    Like a star, shines out her face,
And the form his strong arm presses
    Is sylph like in its grace.
As a leaf on the bounding river
    Is lost in the seething sea,
I know that forever and ever
    My dream is lost to me.

And still the viols are playing
    That grand old wordless rhyme;
And still those two ate swaying
    In perfect tune and time.
If the great bassoons that mutter,
    If the clarinets that blow,
Were given a voice to utter
    The secret things they know,

Would the lists of the slam who slumber
    On the Danube's battle-plains
The unknown hosts outnumber
    Who die 'neath the "Danube's" strains?
Those fall where cannons rattle,
    'Mid the rain of shot and shell;
But these, in a fiercer battle,
    Find death in the music's swell.

With the river's roar of passion
    Is blended the dying groan;
But here, in the halls of fashion,
    Hearts break, and make no moan.
And the music, swelling and sweeping,
    Like the river, knows it all;
But none are counting or keeping
    The lists of these who fall.

"THEY DRIFT DOWN THE HALL TOGETHER"

ANSWERED.

Goodbye—yes, I am going.
    Sudden? Well, you are right;
But a startling truth came home to me
    With sudden force last night.
What is it? Shall I tell you?
    Nay, that is why I go.
I am running away from the battlefield
    Turning my back on the foe.

Riddles? You think me cruel!
    Have you not been most kind?
Why, when you question me like that,
    What answer can I find?
You fear you failed to amuse me,
    Your husband's friend and guest,
Whom he bade you entertain and please—
    Well, you have done your best.
Then why am I going?
    A friend of mine abroad,
Whose theories I have been acting upon,
    Has proven himself a fraud.
You have heard me quote from Plato
    A thousand times no doubt;
Well, I have discovered he did not know
    What he was talking about.

You think I am speaking strangely?
  You cannot understand?
Well, let me look down into your eyes,
  And let me take your hand.
I am running away from danger;
  I am flying before I fall;
I am going because with heart and soul
  I love you—that is all.
There, now you are white with anger;
  I knew it would be so.
You should not question a man too close
  When he tells you he must go.

THROUGH THE VALLEY.

[AFTER JAMES THOMSON.]

As I came through the Valley of Despair,
 As I came through the valley, on my sight,
 More awful than the darkness of the night,
Shone glimpses of a Past that had been fair,
 And memories of eyes that used to smile,
 And wafts of perfume from a vanished isle,
As I came through the valley.

As I came through the valley I could see,
 As I came through the valley, fair and far,
 As drowning men look up and see a star,
The fading shore of my lost Used-to-be;
 And like an arrow in my heart I heard
 The last sad notes of Hope's expiring bird,
As I came through the valley.

As I came through the valley desolate,
 As I came through the valley, like a beam
 Of lurid lightning I beheld a gleam
Of Love's great eyes that now were full of hate.
 Dear God! Dear God! I could bear all but that;
 But I fell down soul-stricken, dead, thereat,
As I came through the valley.

BUT ONE.

The year has but one June, dear friend;
 The year has but one June;
And when that perfect month doth end,
The robin's song, though loud, though long,
 Seems never quite in tune.

The rose, though still its blushing face
 By bee and bird is seen,
May yet have lost that subtle grace—
That nameless spell the winds know
 Which makes it garden's queen.

Life's perfect June, love's red, red rose,
 Have burned and bloomed for me.
Though still youth's summer sunlight glows;
Though thou art kind, dear friend, I find
 I have no heart for thee.

A JUNE ROSE

GUILO.

Yes, yes! I love thee, Guilo; thee alone.
    Why dost thou sigh, and wear that face of sorrow?
The sunshine is today's, although it shone
    On yesterday, and may shine on tomorrow.

I love but thee, my Guilo! be content;
    The greediest heart can claim but present pleasure.
The future is thy God's. The past is spent.
    Today is thine; clasp close the precious treasure.

See how I love thee, Guilo! Lips and eyes
    Could never under thy fond gaze dissemble.
I could not feign these passion-laden sighs;
    Deceiving thee, my pulses would not tremble.

"So I loved Romney." Hush, thou foolish one—
    I should forget him wholly wouldst thou let me;
Or but remember that his day was done
    From that supremest hour when first I met thee.

"And Paul?" Well, what of Paul? Paul had blue eyes,
    And Romney gray, and thine are darkly tender!
One finds fresh feelings under change of skies—
    A new horizon brings a newer splendor.

As I love thee I never loved before;
    Believe me, Guilo, for I speak most truly.
What though to Romney and to Paul I swore
    The self-same words; my heart now worships newly.

We never feel the same emotion twice:
    No two ships ever ploughed the self-same billow;
The waters change with every fall and rise;
    So, Guilo, go contented to thy pillow.

THE DUET.

I was smoking a cigarette;
  Maud, my wife, and the tenor, McKey,
Were singing together a blithe duet,
And days it were better I should forget
  Came suddenly back to me—
Days when life seemed a gay masque ball,
And to love and be loved was the sum of it all.

As they sang together, the whole scene fled,
  The room's rich hangings, the sweet home air,
Stately Maud, with her proud blond head,
And I seemed to see in her place instead
  A wealth of blue-black hair,
And a face, ah! your face—yours, Lisette;
A face it were wiser I should forget.

We were back—well, no matter when or where;
  But you remember, I know, Lisette.
I saw you, dainty and debonair,
With the very same look that you used to wear
  In the days I should forget.
And your lips, as red as the vintage we quaffed,
Were pearl-edged bumpers of wine when you laughed.

Two small slippers with big rosettes
    Peeped out under your kilt skirt there,
While we sat smoking our cigarettes
(Oh, I shall be dust when my heart forgets')
    And singing that self-same an,
And between the verses, for interlude,
I kissed your throat and your shoulders nude.

You were so full of a subtle file,
    You were so warm and so sweet, Lisette;
You were everything men admire,
And there were no fetters to make us tire,
    For you were—a pretty grisette.
But you loved, as only such natures can,
With a love that makes heaven or hell for a man.

* * * * *

They have ceased singing that old duet,
    Stately Maud and the tenor, McKey.
"You are burning your coat with your cigarette,
And *qu' avez vous*, dearest, your lids are wet,"
    Maud says, as she leans o'er me.
And I smile, and lie to her, husband-wise,
"Oh, it is nothing but smoke in my eyes."

"I LOVE THEE; THEE ALONE"

LITTLE QUEEN.

Do you remember the name I wore—
    The old pet-name of Little Queen—
In the dear, dead days that are no more,
    The happiest days of our lives, I ween?
For we loved with that passionate love of youth
    That blesses but once with its perfect bliss—
A love that, in spite of its trust and truth,
    Seems never to thrive in a world like this.

I lived for you, and you lived for me;
    All was centered in "Little Queen;"
And never a thought in our hearts had we
    That strife or trouble could come between.
What utter sinking of self it was!
    How little we cared for the world of men!
For love's fair kingdom and love's sweet laws
    Were all of the world and life to us then.

But a love like ours was a challenge to Fate;
    She rang down the curtain and shifted the scene;
Yet sometimes now, when the day grows late,
    I can hear you calling for Little Queen;

For a happy home and a busy life
     Can never wholly crowd out our past;
In the twilight pauses that come from strife,
     You will think of me while life shall last.

And however sweet the voice of fame
     May sing to me of a great world's praise,
I shall long sometimes for the old pet-name
     That you gave to me in the dear, dead days;
And nothing the angel band can say,
     When I reach the shores of the great Unseen,
Can please me so much as on that day
     To hear your greeting of "Little Queen."

"THAT BLESSES BUT ONCE WITH
ITS PERFECT BLISS"

WHEREFORE?

Wherefore in dreams are sorrows borne anew,
    A healed wound opened, or the past revived?
Last night in my deep sleep I dreamed of you;
    Again the old love woke in me, and thrived
On looks of fire, and kisses, and sweet words
    Like silver waters purling in a stream,
Or like the amorous melodies of birds:
        A dream—a dream!

Again upon the glory of the scene
    There settled that dread shadow of the cross
That, when hearts love too well, falls in between;
    That warns them of impending woe and loss.
Again I saw you drifting from my life,
    As barques are rudely parted in a stream;
Again my heart was torn with awful strife:
        A dream—a dream!

Again the deep night settled on me there,
    Alone I groped, and heard strange waters roll,
Lost in that blackness of supreme despair
    That comes but once to any living soul.

Alone, afraid, I called your name aloud—
　　Mine eyes, unveiled, beheld white stars agleam,
And lo! awake, I cried, "Thank God, thank God!
　　　　A dream—a dream!"

DELILAH.

In the midnight of darkness and terror,
    When I would grope nearer to God,
With my back to a record of error
    And the highway of sin I have trod,
There come to me shapes I would banish—
    The shapes of the deeds I have done;
And I pray and I plead till they vanish—
    All vanish and leave me, save one.

That one with a smile like the splendor
    Of the sun in the middle-day skies—
That one with a spell that is tender—
    That one with a dream in her eyes—
Cometh close, in her rare Southern beauty,
    Her languor, her indolent grace;
And my soul turns its back on its duty,
    To live in the light of her face.

She touches my cheek, and I quiver—
    I tremble with exquisite pains;
She sighs—like an overcharged river
    My blood rushes on through my veins',

She smiles—and in mad-tiger fashion,
  As a she-tiger fondles her own,
I clasp her with fierceness and passion,
  And kiss her with shudder and groan.

Once more, in our love's sweet beginning,
  I put away God and the World;
Once more, in the joys of our sinning,
  Are the hopes of eternity hurled.
There is nothing my soul lacks or misses
  As I clasp the dream shape to my breast;
In the passion and pain of her kisses
  Life blooms to its richest and best.

O ghost of dead sin unrelenting,
  Go back to the dust and the sod!
Too dear and too sweet for repenting,
  Ye stand between me and my God.
If I, by the Throne, should behold you,
  Smiling up with those eyes loved so well,
Close, close in my arms I would fold you,
  And drop with you down to sweet Hell!

DELILAH

LOVE SONG.

Once in the world's first prime,
    When nothing lived or stirred—
Nothing but new-born Time,
    Nor was there even a bird—
The Silence spoke to a Star;
    But I do not dare repeat
What it said to its love afar,
    It was too sweet, too sweet.

But there, in the fair world's youth,
    Ere sorrow had drawn breath,
When nothing was known but Truth,
    Nor was there even death,
The Star to Silence was wed,
    And the Sun was priest that day,
And they made their bridal-bed
    High in the Milky Way.

For the great white star had heard
    Her silent lover's speech;
It needed no passionate word
    To pledge them each to each.

Oh, lady fair and far,
 Hear, oh, hear and apply!
Thou, the beautiful Star—
 The voiceless Silence, I.

TIME AND LOVE.

Time flies. The swift hours hurry by
    And speed us on to untried ways;
New seasons ripen, perish, die,
    And yet love stays.
The old, old love—like sweet, at first,
    At last like bitter wine—
I know not if it blest or curst
    Thy life and mine.

Time flies. In vain our prayers, our tears!
    We cannot tempt him to delays;
Down to the past he bears the years,
    And yet love stays.
Through changing task and varying dream
    We hear the same refrain,
As one can hear a plaintive theme
    Run through each strain.

Time flies. He steals our pulsing youth;
    He robs us of our care-free days;
He takes away our trust and truth:
    And yet love stays.

O Time! take love! When love is vain,
　　When all its best joys die—
When only its regrets remain—
　　Let love, too, fly.

TIME AND LOVE

CHANGE.

Changed? Yes, I will confess it—I have changed.
    I do not love in the old fond way.
I am your friend still—time has not estranged
    One kindly feeling of that vanished day.

But the bright glamour which made life a dream,
    The rapture of that time, its sweet content,
Like visions of a sleeper's brain they seem—
    And yet I cannot tell you how they went.

Why do you gaze with such accusing eyes
    Upon me, dear? Is it so very strange
That hearts, like all things underneath God's skies
    Should sometimes feel the influence of change?

The birds, the flowers, the foliage of the trees,
    The stars which seem so fixed and so sublime,
Vast continents and the eternal seas—
    All these do change with ever-changing time.

The face our mirror shows us year on year
    Is not the same; our dearest aim or need,
Our lightest thought or feeling, hope or fear,
    All, all the law of alteration heed.

How can we ask the human heart to stay
    Content with fancies of Youth's earliest hours?
The year outgrows the violets of May,
    Although, maybe, there are no fairer flowers.

And life may hold no sweeter love than this,
    Which lies so cold, so voiceless, and so dumb.
And shall I miss it, dear? Why, yes, we miss
    The violets always—till the roses come!

DESOLATION.

I think that the bitterest sorrow or pain
    Of love unrequited, or cold death's woe,
    Is sweet compared to that hour when we know
That some grand passion is on the wane;

When we see that the glory and glow and grace
    Which lent a splendor to night and day
    Are surely fading, and showing the gray
And dull groundwork of the commonplace;

When fond expressions on dull ears fall,
    When the hands clasp calmly without one thrill,
    When we cannot muster by force of will
The old emotions that came at call;

When the dream has vanished we fain would keep,
    When the heart, like a watch, runs out of gear,
    And all the savor goes out of the year,
Oh, then is the time—if we can—to weep!

But no tears soften this dull, pale woe;
    We must sit and face it with dry, sad eyes.
    If we seek to hold it, the swifter joy flies—
We can only be passive, and let it go.

ISAURA.

Dost thou not tire, Isaura, of this play?
    "What play?" Why, this old play of winning hearts!
Nay, now, lift not thine eyes in that feigned way:
    'Tis all in vain—I know thee and thine arts.

Let us be frank, Isaura. I have made
    A study of thee; and while I admire
The practised skill with which thy plans are laid,
    I can but wonder if thou dost not tire.

Why, I tire even of Hamlet and Macbeth!
    When overlong the season runs, I find
Those master-scenes of passion, blood, and death,
    After a time do pall upon my mind.

Dost thou not tire of lifting up thine eyes
    To read the story thou hast read so oft—
Of ardent glances and deep quivering sighs,
    Of haughty faces suddenly grown soft?

Is it not stale, oh, very stale, to thee,
    The scene that follows? Hearts are much the same;
The loves of men but vary in degree—
    They find no new expressions for the flame.

Thou must know all they utter ere they speak,
    As I know Hamlet's part, whoever plays.
Oh, does it not seem sometimes poor and weak?
    I think thou must grow weary of their ways.

I pity thee, Isaura! I would be
    The humblest maiden with her dream untold
Rather than live a Queen of Hearts, like thee,
    And find life's rarest treasures stale and old.

I pity thee; for now, let come what may,
    Fame, glory, riches, yet life will lack all.
Wherewith can salt be salted? And what way
    Can life be seasoned after love doth pall?

THE COQUETTE.

Alone she sat with her accusing heart,
    That, like a restless comrade frightened sleep,
And every thought that found her, left a dart
    That hurt her so, she could not even weep.

Her heart that once had been a cup well filled
    With love's red wine, save for some drops of gall
She knew was empty; though it had not spilled
    Its sweets for one, but wasted them on all.

She stood upon the grave of her dead truth,
    And saw her soul's bright armor red with rust,
And knew that all the riches of her youth
    Were Dead Sea apples, crumbling into dust.

Love that had turned to bitter, biting scorn,
    Hearthstones despoiled, and homes made desolate,
Made her cry out that she was ever born,
    To loathe her beauty and to curse her fate.

TIRED OF THE OFT-READ STORY

NEW AND OLD.

I and new love, in all its living bloom,
    Sat vis-a-vis, while tender twilight hours
    Went softly by us, treading as on flowers.
Then suddenly I saw within the room
The old love, long since lying in its tomb.
    It dropped the cerecloth from its fleshless face
    And smiled on me, with a remembered grace
That, like the noontide, lit the gloaming's gloom.

Upon its shroud there hung the grave's green mould,
    About it hung the odor of the dead;
    Yet from its cavernous eyes such light was shed
That all my life seemed gilded, as with gold;
    Unto the trembling new love "'Go," I said
"I do not need thee, for I have the old."

NOT QUITE THE SAME.

Not quite the same the spring-time seems to me,
    Since that sad season when in separate ways
    Our paths diverged. There are no more such days
As dawned for us in that lost time when we
    Dwelt in the realm of dreams, illusive dreams;
    Spring may be just as fair now, but it seems
        Not quite the same.

Not quite the same is life, since we two parted,
    Knowing it best to go our ways alone.
    Fair measures of success we both have known,
And pleasant hours, and yet something departed
    Which gold, nor fame, nor anything we win
    Can all replace. And either life has been
        Not quite the same.

Love is not quite the same, although each heart
    Has formed new ties that are both sweet and true,
    But that wild rapture, which of old we knew,
Seems to have been a something set apart
    With that lost dream. There is no passion, now,
    Mixed with this later love, which seems, somehow,
        Not quite the same.

Not quite the same am I. My inner being
  Reasons and knows that all is for the best.
  Yet vague regrets stir always in my breast,
As my soul's eyes turn sadly backward, seeing
  The vanished self that evermore must be,
  This side of what we call eternity,
    Not quite the same.

FROM THE GRAVE.

When the first sere leaves of the year were falling,
      I heard, with a heart that was strangely thrilled,
Out of the grave of a dead Past calling,
      A voice I fancied forever stilled.

All through winter and spring and summer,
            Silence hung over that grave like a pall,
But, borne on the breath of the last sad comer,
      I listen again to the old-time call.

It is only a love of a by-gone season,
      A senseless folly that mocked at me
A reckless passion that lacked all reason,
      So I killed it, and hid it where none could see.

I smothered it first to stop its crying,
      Then stabbed it through with a good sharp blade,
And cold and pallid I saw it lying,
      And deep—ah' deep was the grave I made.

But now I know that there is no killing
      A thing like Love, for it laughs at Death.
There is no hushing, there is no stilling
      That which is part of your life and breath.

You may bury it deep, and leave behind you
    The land, the people, that knew your slain;
It will push the sods from its grave, and find you
    On wastes of water or desert plain.

You may hear but tongues of a foreign people,
    You may list to sounds that are strange and new;
But, clear as a silver bell in a steeple,
    That voice from the grave shall call to you.

You may rouse your pride, you may use your reason.
    And seem for a space to slay Love so;
But, all in its own good time and season,
    It will rise and follow wherever you go.

You shall sit sometimes, when the leaves are falling,
    Alone with your heart, as I sit today,
And hear that voice from your dead Past calling
    Out of the graves that you hid away.

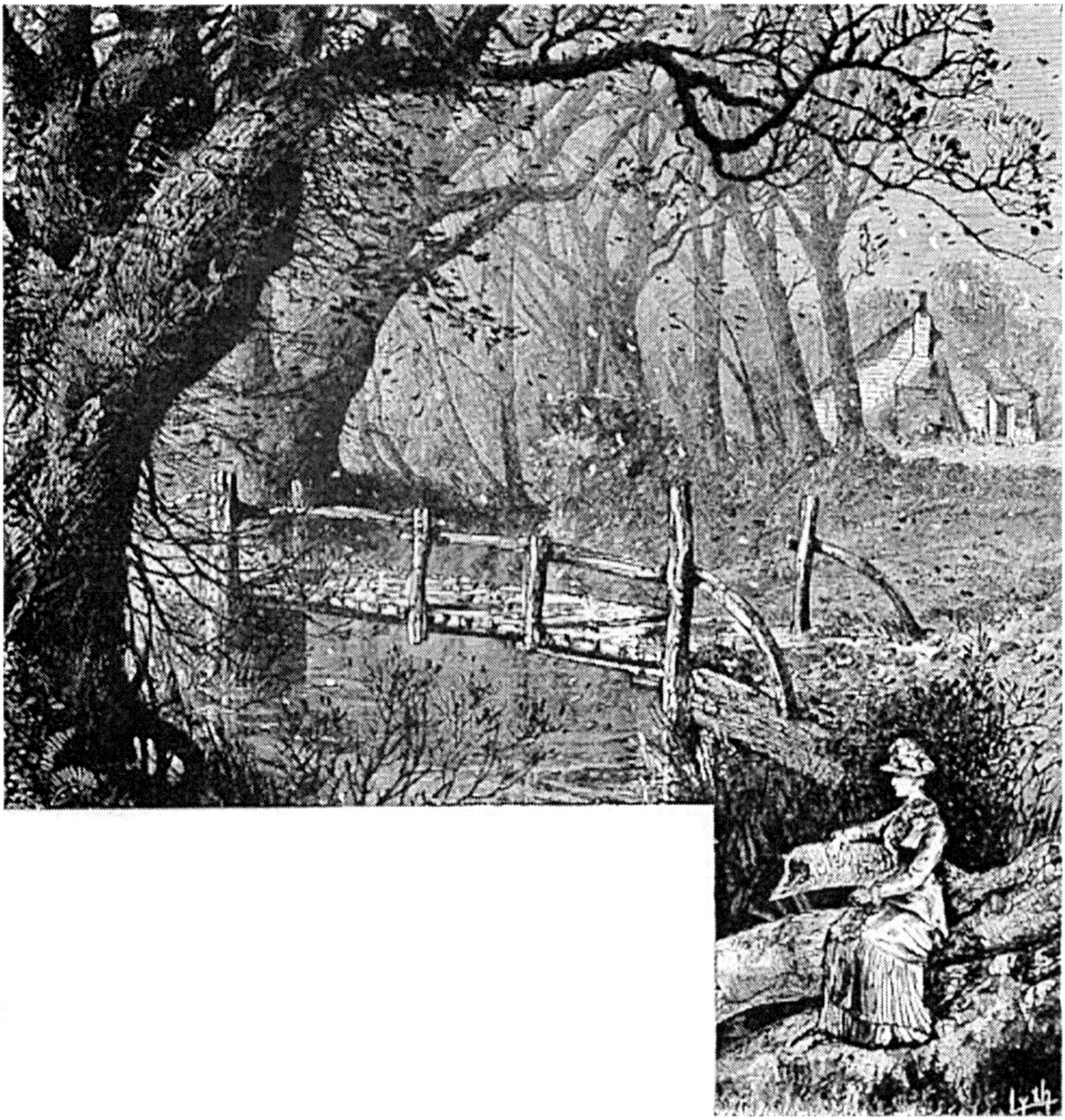

A WALTZ-QUADRILLE.

The band was playing a waltz-quadrille,
    I felt as light as a wind-blown feather,
As we floated away, at the caller's will,
    Through the intricate, mazy dance together.
Like mimic armies our lines were meeting,
Slowly advancing, and then retreating,
    All decked in their bright array;
And back and forth to the music's rhyme
We moved together, and all the time
    I knew you were going away.

The fold of your strong arm sent a thrill
    From heart to brain as we gently glided
Like leaves on the wave of that waltz-quadrille;
    Parted, met, and again divided—
You drifting one way, and I another,
Then suddenly turning and facing each other,
    Then off in the blithe chasse,
Then airily back to our places swaying,
While every beat of the music seemed saying
    That you were going away.

I said to my heart, "Let us take our fill
     Of mirth and music and love and laughter;
For it all must end with this waltz-quadrille,
     And life will be never the same life after.
Oh, that the caller might go on calling,
Oh, that the music might go on falling
     Like a shower of silver spray,
While we whirled on to the vast Forever,
Where no hearts break, and no ties sever,
     And no one goes away."

A clamor, a crash, and the band was still;
     'Twas the end of the dream, and the end of the measure:
The last low notes of that waltz-quadrille
     Seemed like a dirge o'er the death of Pleasure.
You said goodnight, and the spell was over—
Too warm for a friend, and too cold for a lover—
     There was nothing else to say;
But the lights looked dim, and the dancers weary,
And the music was sad, and the hall was dreary,
     After you went away.

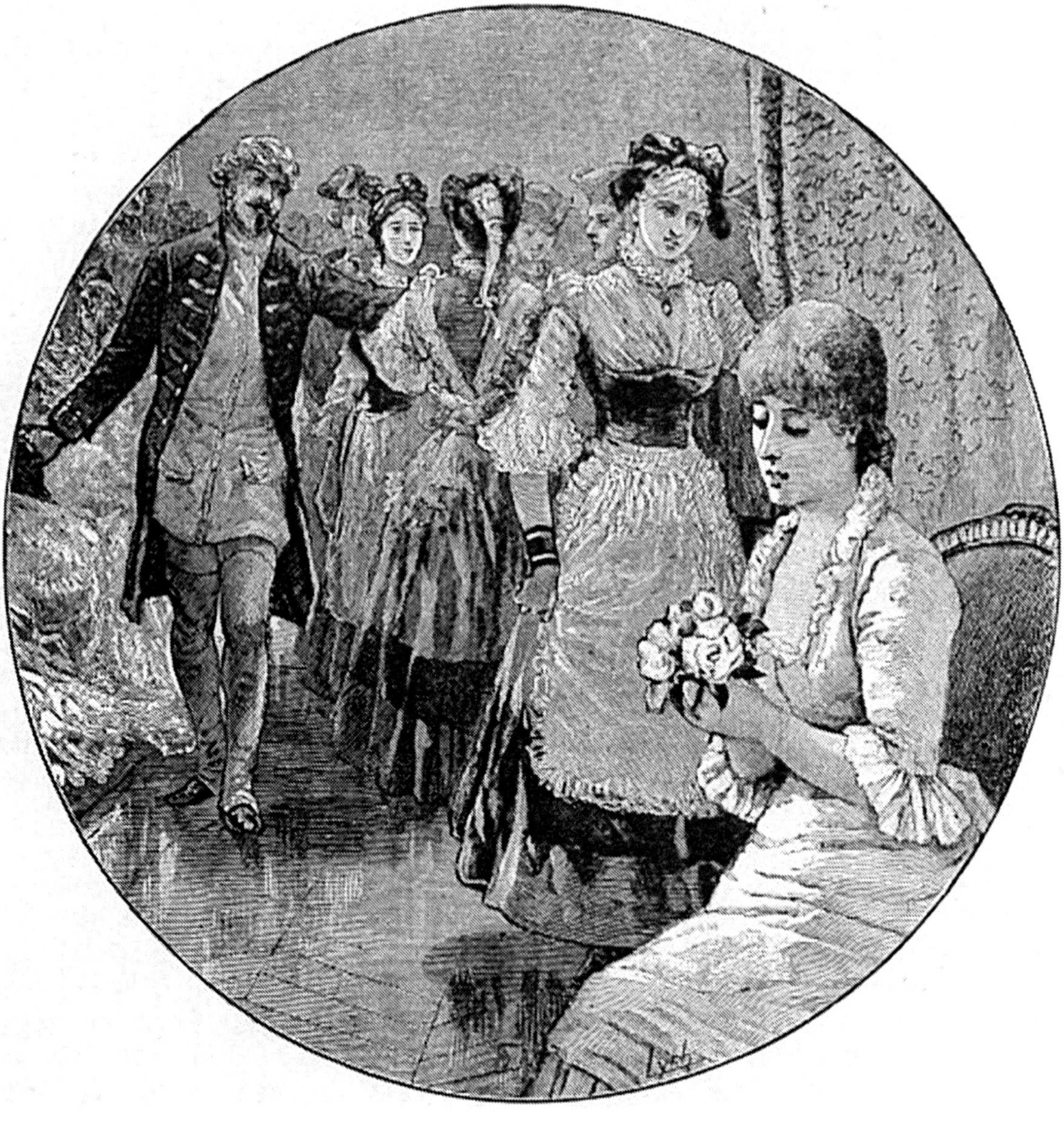

BEPPO.

Why art thou sad, my Beppo? But last eve,
    Here at my feet, thy dear head on my breast,
I heard thee say thy heart would no more grieve
    Or feel the olden ennui and unrest.

What troubles thee? Am I not all thine own?—
    I, so long sought, so sighed for and so dear?
And do I not live but for thee alone?
    "Thou hast seen Lippo, whom I loved last year!"

Well, what of that? Last year is naught to me—
    'Tis swallowed in the ocean of the past.
Art thou not glad 'twas Lippo, and not thee,
    Whose brief bright day in that great gulf was cast.
Thy day is all before thee. Let no cloud,
    Here in the very morn of our delight,
Drift up from distant foreign skies, to shroud
    Our sun of love whose radiance is so bright.

"Thou art not first?" Nay, and he who would be
    Defeats his own heart's dearest purpose then.
No truer truth was ever told to thee—
    Who has loved most, he best can love again.

If Lippo (and not he alone) has taught
    The arts that please thee, wherefore art thou sad?
Since all my vast love-lore to thee is brought,
    Look up and smile, my Beppo, and be glad.

TIRED.

I am tired tonight, and something,
    The wind maybe, or the rain,
Or the cry of a bird in the copse outside,
    Has brought back the past and its pain.
And I feel, as I sit here thinking,
    That the hand of a dead old June
Has reached out hold of my heart's loose strings,
    And is drawing them up in tune.

I am tired tonight, and I miss you,
    And long for you, love, through tears;
And it seems but today that I saw you go—
    You, who have been gone for years.
And I seem to be newly lonely—
    I, who am so much alone;
And the strings of my heart are well in tune,
    But they have not the same old tone.

I am tired; and that old sorrow
    Sweeps down the bed of my soul,
As a turbulent river might sudden'y break
    way from a dam's control.
It beareth a wreck on its bosom,
    A wreck with a snow-white sail;
And the hand on my heart strings thrums away,
    But they only respond with a wail.

"THE BURDEN OF DEAR HUMAN TIES"

THE SPEECH OF SILENCE.

The solemn Sea of Silence lies between us;
 I know thou livest, and them lovest me,
And yet I wish some white ship would come sailing
 Across the ocean, beating word from thee.

The dead calm awes me with its awful stillness.
 No anxious doubts or fears disturb my breast;
I only ask some little wave of language,
 To stir this vast infinitude of rest.

I am oppressed with this great sense of loving;
 So much I give, so much receive from thee;
Like subtle incense, rising from a censer,
 So floats the fragrance of thy love round me.

All speech is poor, and written words unmeaning;
 Yet such I ask, blown hither by some wind,
To give relief to this too perfect knowledge,
 The Silence so impresses on my mind.

How poor the love that needeth word or message,
 To banish doubt or nourish tenderness!
I ask them but to temper love's convictions
 The Silence all too fully doth express.

Too deep the language which the spirit utters;
    Too vast the knowledge which my soul hath stirred.
Send some white ship across the Sea of Silence,
    And interrupt its utterance with a word.

CONVERSION.

I have lived this life as the skeptic lives it;
    I have said the sweetness was less than the gall;
Praising, nor cursing, the Hand that gives it,
    I have drifted aimlessly through it all.
I have scoffed at the tale of a so-called heaven;
    I have laughed at the thought of a Supreme Friend;
I have said that it only to man was given
    To live, to endure; and to die was the end.

But I know that a good God reigneth,
    Generous-hearted and kind and true;
Since unto a worm like me he deigneth
    To send so royal a gift as you.
Bright as a star you gleam on my bosom,
    Sweet as a rose that the wild bee sips;
And I know, my own, my beautiful blossom,
    That none but a God could mould such lips.

And I believe, in the fullest measure
    That ever a strong man's heart could hold,
In all the tales of heavenly pleasure
    By poets sung or by prophets told;

For in the joy of your shy, sweet kisses,
    Your pulsing touch and your languid sigh
I am filled and thrilled with better blisses
    Than ever were claimed for souls on high.

And now I have faith in all the stories
    Told of the beauties of unseen lands;
Of royal splendors and marvellous glories
    Of the golden city not made with hands
For the silken beauty of falling tresses,
    Of lips all dewy and cheeks aglow,
With—what the mind in a half trance guesses
    Of the twin perfection of drifts of snow;

Of limbs like marble, of thigh and shoulder
    Carved like a statue in high relief—
These, as the eyes and the thoughts grow bolder,
    Leave no room for an unbelief.
So my lady, my queen most royal,
    My skepticism has passed away;
If you are true to me, true and loyal,
    I will believe till the Judgment-day.

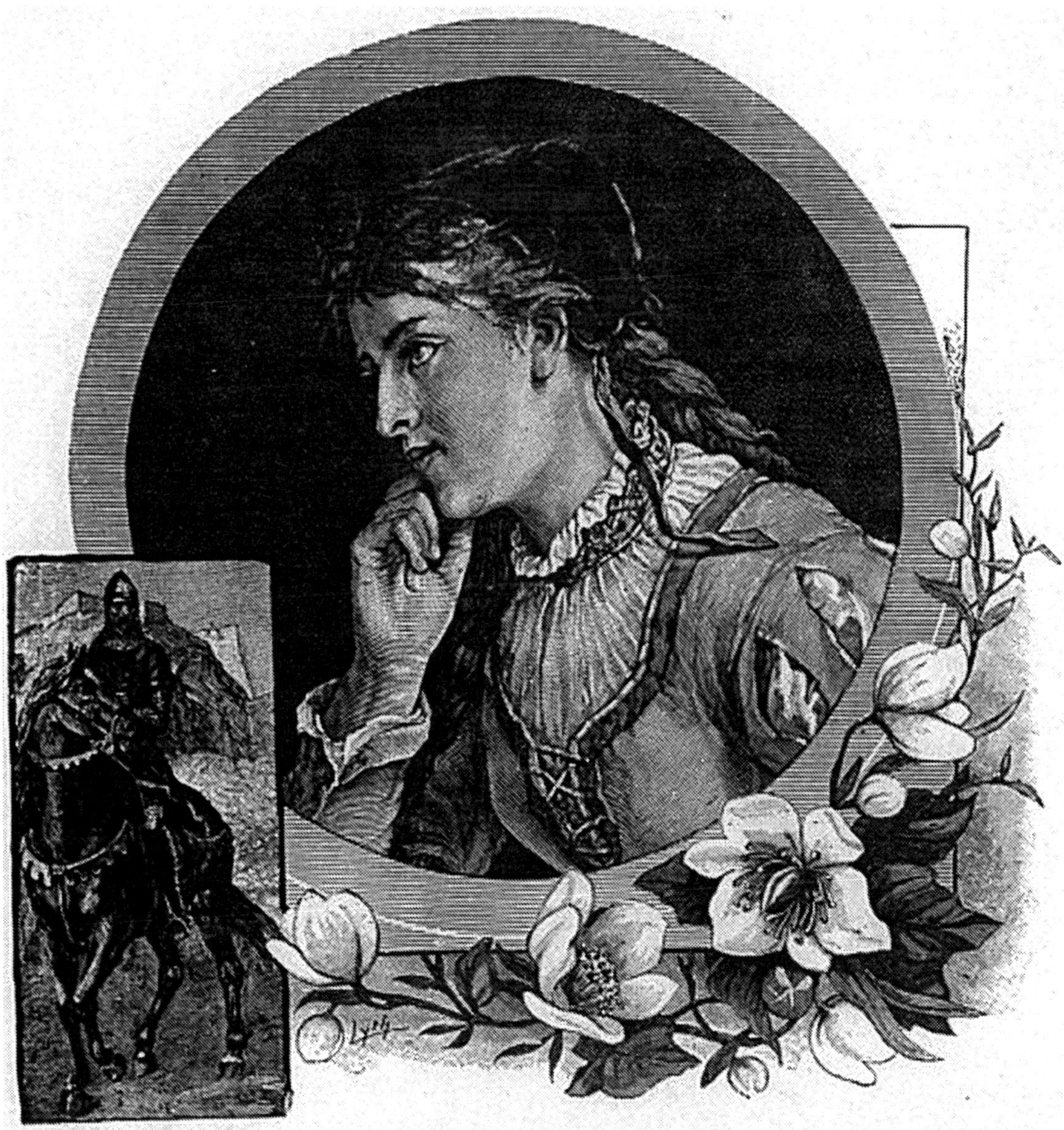

LOVE'S COMING.

She had looked for his coming as warriors come,
    With the clash of arms and the bugle's call:
But he came instead with a stealthy tread,
    Which she did not hear at all.

She had thought how his armor would blaze in the sun,
    As he rode like a prince to claim his bride:
In the sweet dim light of the falling night
    She found him at her side.

She had dreamed how the gaze of his strange, bold eye
    Would wake her heart to a sudden glow:
She found in his face the familiar grace
    Of a friend she used to know.

She had dreamed how his coming would stir her soul,
    As the ocean is stirred by the wild storm's strife:
He brought her the balm of a heavenly calm,
    And a peace which crowned her life.

OLD AND NEW.

Long have the poets vaunted, in their lays,
    Old times, old loves, old friendship, and old wine.
Why should the old monopolize all praise?
    Then let the new claim mine.

Give me strong new friends when the old prove weak
    Or fail me in my darkest hour of need;
Why perish with the ship that springs a leak
    Or lean upon a reed?

Give me new love, warm, palpitating, sweet,
    When all the grace and beauty leave the old;
When like a rose it withers at my feet,
    Or like a hearth grows cold.

Give me new times, bright with a prosperous cheer,
    In place of old, tear-blotted, burdened days;
I hold a sunlit present far more dear,
    And worthy of my praise.

When the old deeds are threadbare and worn through,
    And all too narrow for the broadening soul,
Give me the fine, firm texture of the new,
    Fair, beautiful, and whole!

PERFECTNESS.

All perfect things are saddening in effect.
    The autumn wood robed in its scarlet clothes,
    The matchless tinting on the royal rose
Whose velvet leaf by no least flaw is flecked,
Love's supreme moment, when the soul unchecked
    Soars high as heaven, and its best rapture knows—
    These hold a deeper pathos than our woes,
Since they leave nothing better to expect.

Resistless change, when powerless to improve,
    Can only mar. The gold will pale to gray;
    Nothing remains tomorrow as today;
The lose will not seem quite so fait, and love
    Must find its measures of delight made less.
    Ah, how imperfect is all Perfectness!

LOVE AND LIFE

ATTRACTION.

The meadow and the mountain with desire
    Gazed on each other, till a fierce unrest
    Surged 'neath the meadow's seemingly calm breast,
And all the mountain's fissures ran with fire.

A mighty river rolled between them there.
    What could the mountain do but gaze and burn?
    What could the meadow do but look and yearn,
And gem its bosom to conceal despair?

Their seething passion agitated space,
    Till, lo! the lands a sudden earthquake shook,
    The river fled, the meadow leaped and took
The leaning mountain in a close embrace.

GRACIA.

Nay, nay, Antonio! nay, thou shalt not blame her,
    My Gracia, who hath so deserted me.
Thou art my friend, but if thou dost defame her
    I shall not hesitate to challenge thee.

"Curse and forget her?" So I might another,
    One not so bounteous-natured or so fair;
But she, Antonio, she was like no other—
    I curse her not, because she was so rare.

She was made out of laughter and sweet kisses;
    Not blood, but sunshine, through her blue veins ran
Her soul spilled over with its wealth of blisses;
    She was too great for loving but a man.

None but a god could keep so rare a creature:
    I blame her not for her inconstancy;
When I recall each radiant smile and feature,
    I wonder she so long was true to me.

Call her not false or fickle. I, who love her,
    Do hold her not unlike the royal sun,
That, all unmated, roams the wide world over
    And lights all worlds, but lingers not with one.

If she were less a goddess, more a woman,
    And so had dallied for a time with me,
And then had left me, I, who am but human,
    Would slay her and her newer love, maybe.

But since she seeks Apollo, or another
    Of those lost gods (and seeks him all in vain)
And has loved me as well as any other
    Of her men loves, why, I do not complain.

AD FINEM.

On the white throat of the' useless passion
    That scorched my soul with its burning breath
I clutched my fingers in murderous fashion,
    And gathered them close in a grip of death;
For why should I fan, or feed with fuel,
    A love that showed me but blank despair?
So my hold was firm, and my grasp was cruel—
    I meant to strangle it then and there!

I thought it was dead. But with no warning,
    It rose from its grave last night, and came
And stood by my bed till the early morning,
    And over and over it spoke your name.
Its throat was red where my hands had held it;
    It burned my brow with its scorching breath;
And I said, the moment my eyes beheld it,
    "A love like this can know no death."

For just one kiss that your lips have given
    In the lost and beautiful past to me
I would gladly barter my hopes of Heaven
    And all the bliss of Eternity.

For never a joy are the angels keeping,
    To lay at my feet in Paradise,
Like that of into your strong arms creeping,
    And looking into your love-lit eyes.

I know, in the way that sins are reckoned,
    This thought is a sin of the deepest dye;
But I know, too, if an angel beckoned,
    Standing close by the Throne on High,
And you, adown by the gates infernal,
    Should open your loving arms and smile,
I would turn my back on things supernal,
    To lie on your breast a little while.

To know for an hour you were mine completely—
    Mine in body and soul, my own—
I would bear unending tortures sweetly,
    With not a murmur and not a moan.
A lighter sin or a lesser error
    Might change through hope or fear divine;
But there is no fear, and hell has no terror,
    To change or alter a love like mine.

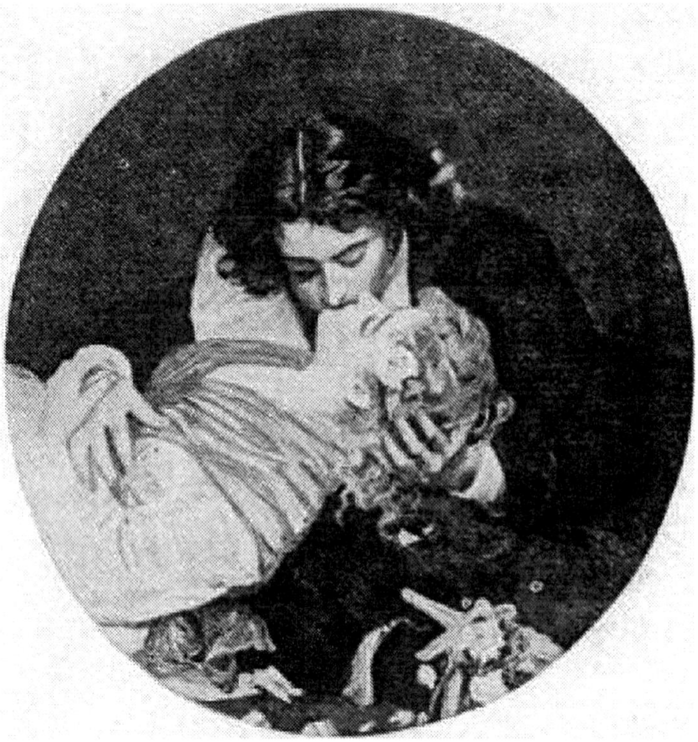

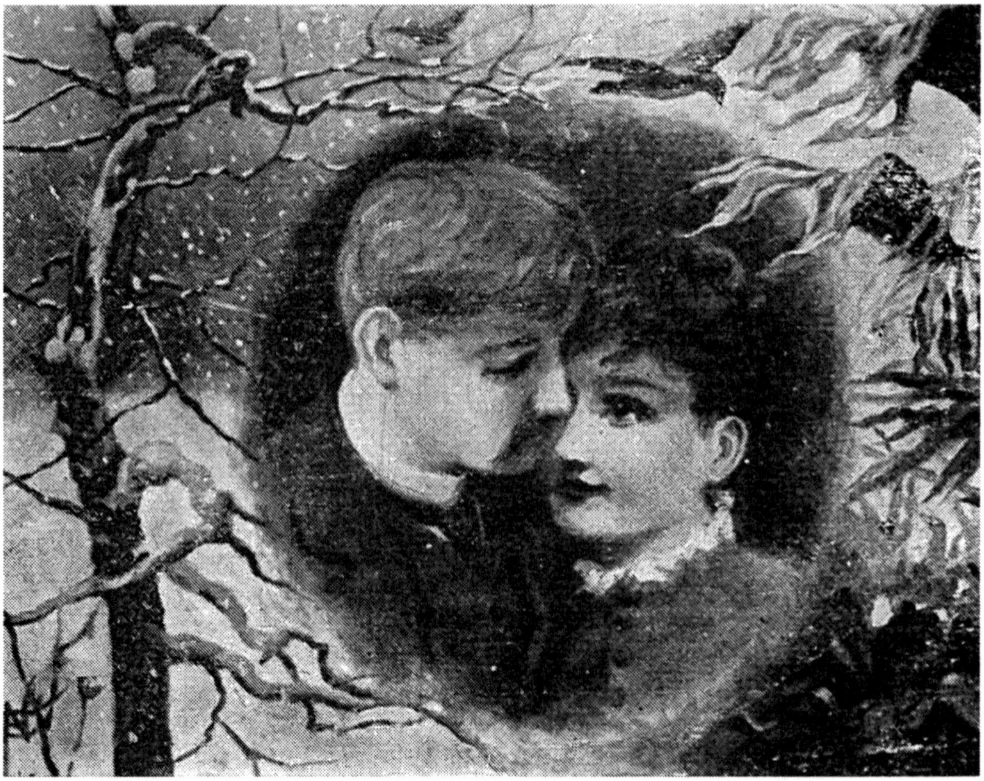

BLEAK WEATHER.

Dear Love, where the red lilies blossomed and grew
    The white snows are falling;
And all through the woods where I wandered with you
    The loud winds are calling;
And the robin that piped to us tune upon tune,
    Neath the oak, you remember,
O'er hill-top and forest has followed the June
    And left us December.

He has left like a friend who is true in the sun
    And false in the shadows;
He has found new delights in the land where he's gone,
    Greener woodlands and meadows.
Let him go! what care we? let the snow shroud the lea,
    Let it drift on the heather;
We can sing through it all: I have you, you have me.
    And we'll laugh at the weather.

The old year may die and a new year be born
    That is bleaker and colder:
It cannot dismay us; we dare it, we scorn,
    For our love makes us bolder.
Ah, Robin! sing loud on your far distant lea,
    You friend in fair weather!
But here is a song sung that's fuller of glee,
    By two warm hearts together.

AN ANSWER.

If all the year was summer time,
    And all the aim of life
Was just to lilt on like a rhyme,
    Then I would be your wife.

If all the days were August days,
    And crowned with golden weather,
How happy then through green-clad ways
    We two could stray together!

If all the nights were moonlit nights,
    And we had naught to do
But just to sit and plan delights,
    Then I would wed with you.

If life was all a summer fete,
    Its soberest pace the "glide,"
Then I would choose you for my mate,
    And keep you at my side.

But winter makes full half the year,
    And labor half of life,
And all the laughter and good cheer
    Give place to wearing strife.

Days will grow cold, and moons wax old.
    And then a heart that's true
Is better far than grace or gold—
    And so, my love, adieu!
    I cannot wed with you.

YOU WILL FORGET ME.

You will forget me. The years are so tender,
    They bind up the wounds which we think are so deep;
This dream of our youth will fade out as the splendor
    Fades from the skies when the sun sinks to sleep;
The cloud of forgetfulness, over and over
    Will banish the last rosy colors away,
And the fingers of time will weave garlands to cover
    The scar which you think is a life-mark today.

You will forget me. The one boon you covet
    Now above all things will soon seem no prize;
And the heart, which you hold not in keeping to prove it
    True or untrue, will lose worth in your eyes.
The one drop today, that you deem only wanting
    To fill your life-cup to the brim, soon will seem
But a valueless mite; and the ghost that is haunting
    The aisles of your heart will pass out with the dream.

You will forget me; will thank me for saying
    The words which you think are so pointed with pain.
Time loves a new lay; and the dirge he is playing
    Will change for you soon to a livelier strain.
I shall pass from your life—I shall pass out forever,
    And these hours we have spent will be sunk in the past.
Youth buries its dead; grief kills seldom or never,
    And forgetfulness covers all sorrows at last.

THE FAREWELL OF CLARIMONDE.

(Suggested by the "Clarimonde" OF Théophile Gautier.)

Adieu, Romauld! But thou canst not forget me.
    Although no more I haunt thy dreams at night,
Thy hungering heart forever must regret me,
    And starve for those lost moments of delight.

Naught shall avail thy priestly rites and duties,
    Nor fears of Hell, nor hopes of Heaven beyond:
Before the Cross shall rise my fair form's beauties—
    The lips, the limbs, the eyes of Clarimonde.

Like gall the wine sipped from the sacred chalice
    Shall taste to one who knew my red mouth's bliss,
When Youth and Beauty dwelt in Love's own palace,
    And life flowed on in one eternal kiss.

Through what strange ways I come, dear heart, to reach thee,
    From viewless lands, by paths no man e'er trod!
I braved all fears, all dangers dared, to teach thee
    A love more mighty than thy love of God.

Think not in all His Kingdom to discover
    Such joys, Romauld, as ours, when fierce yet fond
I clasped thee—kissed thee—crowned thee my one lover:
    Thou canst not find another Clarimonde.

I knew all arts of love: he who possessed me
    Possessed all women, and could never tire;
A new life dawned for him who once caressed me;
    Satiety itself I set on fire.

Inconstancy I chained: men died to win me;
    Kings cast by crowns for one hour on my breast:
And all the passionate tide of love within me
    I gave to thee, Romauld. Wert thou not blest?

Yet, for the love of God, thy hand hath riven
    Our welded souls. But not in prayer well conned,
Not in thy dearly-purchased peace of Heaven,
    Canst thou forget those hours with Clarimonde.

THE TRIO.

We love but once. The great gold orb of light
    From dawn to even-tide doth cast his ray;
But the full splendor of his perfect might
    Is reached but once throughout the livelong day.

We love but once. The waves, with ceaseless motion,
    Do day and night plash on the pebbled shore;
But the strong tide of the resistless ocean
    Sweeps in but one hour of the twenty-four.

We love but once. A score of times, perchance,
    We may be moved in fancy's fleeting fashion—
May treasure up a word, a tone, a glance;
    But only once we feel the soul's great passion.

We love but once. Love walks with death and birth
    (The saddest, the unkindest of the three);
And only once while we sojourn on earth
    Can that strange trio come to you or me.

MISCELLANEOUS POEMS.

THE LOST GARDEN.

There was a fair green garden sloping
    From the south-east side of the mountain-ledge;
And the earliest tint of the dawn came groping
    Down through its paths, from the day's dim edge.
The bluest skies and the reddest roses
    Arched and varied its velvet sod;
And the glad birds sang, as the soul supposes
    The angels sing on the hills of God.

I wandered there when my veins seemed bursting
    With life's rare rapture and keen delight,
And yet in my heart was a constant thirsting
    For something over the mountain-height.
I wanted to stand in the blaze of glory
    That turned to crimson the peaks of snow,
And the winds from the west all breathed a story
    Of realms and regions I longed to know.

I saw on the garden's south side growing
    The brightest blossoms that breathe of June;
I saw in the east how the sun was glowing,
    And the gold air shook with a wild bird's tune;

I heard the drip of a silver fountain,
    And the pulse of a young laugh throbbed with glee
But still I looked out over the mountain
    Where unnamed wonders awaited me.

I came at last to the western gateway,
    That led to the path I longed to climb;
But a shadow fell on my spirit straightway,
    For close at my side stood gray-beard Time.
I paused, with feet that were fain to linger,
    Hard by that garden's golden gate,
But Time spoke, pointing with one stern finger;
    "Pass on," he said, "for the day groes late."

And now on the chill giay cliffs I wander,
    The heights recede which I thought to find,
And the light seems dim on the mountain yonder,
    When I think of the garden I left behind.
Should I stand at last on its summit's splendor,
    I know full well it would not repay
For the fair lost tints of the dawn so tender
    That crept up over the edge o' day.

I would go back, but the ways are winding,
    If ways there are to that land, in sooth,
For what man succeeds in ever finding
    A path to the garden of his lost youth?
But I think sometimes, when the June stars glisten,
    That a rose scent dufts from far away,
And I know, when I lean from the cliffs and listen,
    That a young laugh breaks on the air like spray.

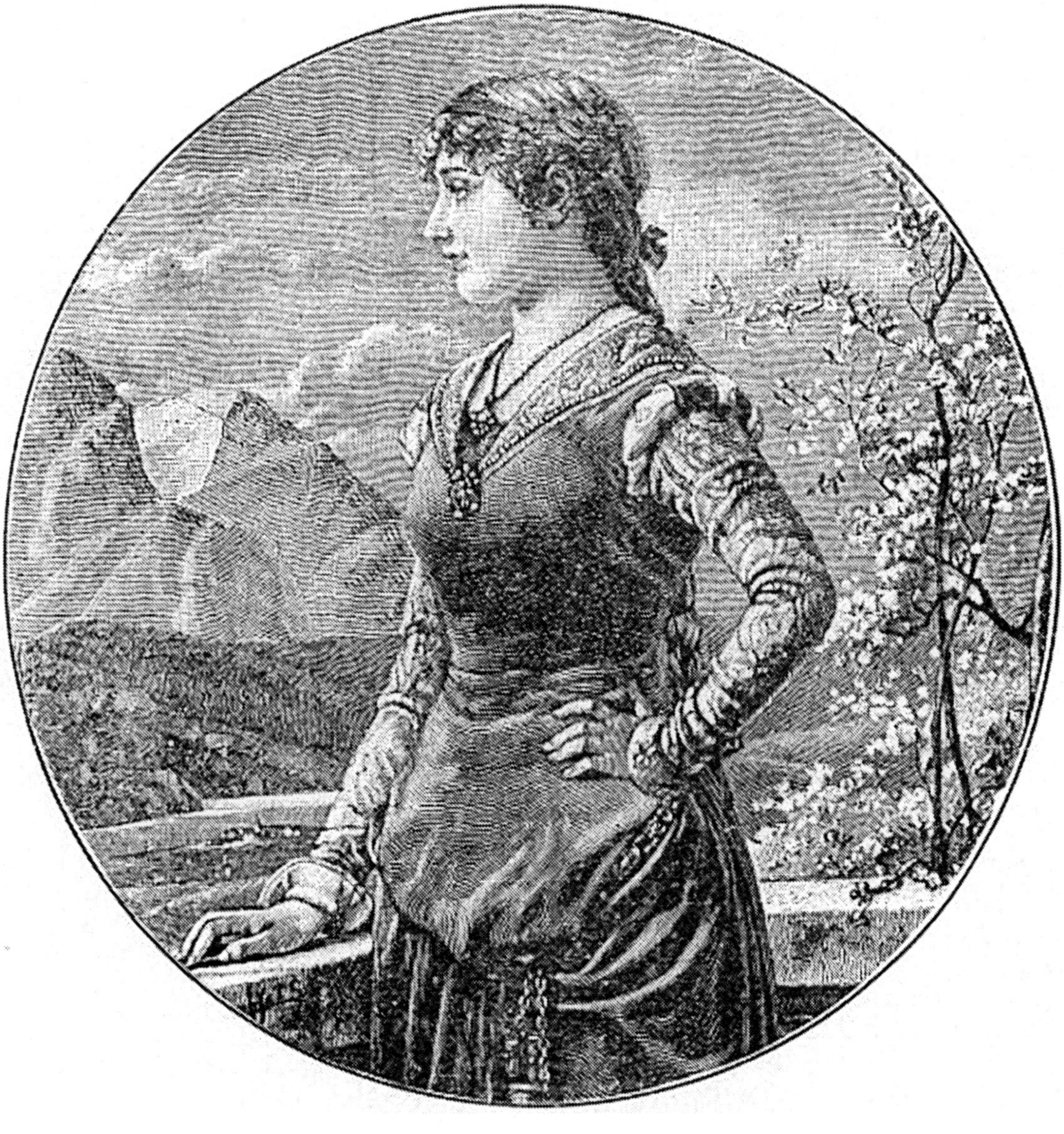

ART AND HEART.

Though critics may bow to art, and I am its own true lover,
It is not art, but *heart*, which wins the wide world over.

Though smooth be the heartless prayer, no ear in Heaven will mind it,
And the finest phrase falls dead if there is no feeling behind it.

Though perfect the player's touch, little, if any, he sways us,
Unless we feel his heart throb through the music he plays us.

Though the poet may spend his life in skilfully rounding a measure,
Unless he writes from a full, warm heart he gives us little pleasure.

So it is not the speech which tells, but the impulse which goes with the
saying;
And it is not the words of the prayer, but the yearning back of the
praying.

It is not the artist's skill which into our soul comes stealing
With a joy that is almost pain, but it is the player's feeling.

And it is not the poet's song, though sweeter than sweet bells chiming,
Which thrills us through and through, but the heart which beats under
the rhyming.

And therefore I say again, though I am art's own true lover,
That it is not art, but heart, which wins the wide world over.

RECOLLECTIONS

MOCKERY.

Why do we grudge our sweets so to the living
    Who, God knows, find at best too much of gall,
And then with generous, open hands kneel, giving
    Unto the dead our all?

Why do we pierce the warm hearts, sin or sorrow,
    With idle jests, or scorn, or cruel sneers,
And when it cannot know, on some tomorrow,
    Speak of its woe through tears?

What do the dead care, for the tender token—
    The love, the praise, the floral offerings?
But palpitating, living hearts are broken
    For want of just these things.

AS BY FIRE.

Sometimes I feel so passionate a yearning
    For spiritual perfection here below,
This vigorous frame, with healthful fervor burning,
    Seems my determined foe,

So actively it makes a stern resistance,
    So cruelly sometimes it wages war
Against a wholly spiritual existence
    Which I am striving for.

It interrupts my soul's intense devotions;
    Some hope it strangles, of divinest birth,
With a swift rush of violent emotions
    Which link me to the earth.

It is as if two mortal foes contended
    Within my bosom in a deadly strife,
One for the loftier aims for souls intended,
    One for the earthly life.

And yet I know this very war within me,
    Which brings out all my will-power and control,
This very conflict at the last shall win me
    The loved and longed-for goal.

The very fire which seems sometimes so cruel
    Is the white light that shows me my own strength.
A furnace, fed by the divinest fuel,
    It may become at length.

Ah! when in the immortal ranks enlisted,
    I sometimes wonder if we shall not find
That not by deeds, but by what we've resisted,
    Our places are assigned.

IF I SHOULD DIE.

RONDEAU.

If I should die, how kind you all would grow!
In that strange hour I would not have one foe.
      There are no words too beautiful to say
      Of one who goes forevermore away
Across that ebbing tide which has no flow.

With what new lustre my good deeds would glow!
If faults were mine, no one would call them so,
      Or speak of me in aught but praise that day,
      If I should die.

Ah, friends! before my listening ear lies low,
While I can hear and understand, bestow
      That gentle treatment and fond love, I pray,
      The lustre of whose late though radiant way
Would gild my grave with mocking light, I know,
      If I should die.

MÉSALLIANCE.

I am troubled tonight with a curious pain;
It is not of the flesh, it is not of the brain,
    Nor yet of a heart that is breaking:
But down still deeper, and out of sight—
In the place where the soul and the body unite—
    There lies the scat of the aching.

They have been lovers in days gone by;
But the soul is fickle, and longs to fly
    From the fettering mesalliance:
And she tears at the bonds which are binding her so,
And pleads with the body to let her go,
    But he will not yield compliance.

For the body loves, as he loved in the past,
When he wedded the soul; and he holds her fast,
    And swears that he will not loose her;
That he will keep her and hide her away
For ever and ever and for a day
    From the arms of Death, the seducer.

Ah! this is the strife that is wearying me—
The strife 'twixt a soul that would be free
    And a body that will not let her.

And I say to my soul, "Be calm, and wait;
For I tell ye truly that soon or late
    Ye surely shall drop each fetter."

And I say to the body, "Be kind, I pray;
For the soul is not of thy mortal clay,
    But is formed in spirit fashion."
And still through the hours of the solemn night
I can hear my sad soul's plea for flight,
    And my body's reply of passion.

DAY DREAMS

RESPONSE.

I said this morning, as I leaned and threw
    My shutters open to the Spring's surprise,
"Tell me, O Earth, how is it that in you
    Year after year the same fresh feelings rise?
How do you keep your young exultant glee?
No more those sweet emotions come to me.

"I note through all your fissures how the tide
    Of healthful life goes leaping as of old;
Your royal dawns retain their pomp and pride;
    Your sunsets lose no atom of their gold.
How can this wonder be?" My soul's fine ear
Leaned, listening, till a small voice answered near:

"My days lapse never over into night;
    My nights encroach not on the rights of dawn.
I rush not breathless after some delight;
    I waste no grief for any pleasure gone.
My July noons burn not the entire year.
Heart, hearken well!" "Yes, yes; go on; I hear."

"I do not strive to make my sunsets' gold
    Pave all the dim and distant realms of space.
I do not bid my crimson dawns unfold
    To lend the midnight a fictitious grace.
I break no law, for all God's laws are good.
Heart, hast thou heard?" "Yes, yes; and understood."

DROUTH.

Why do we pity those who weep? The pain
    That finds a ready outlet in the flow
    Of salt and bitter tears is blessed woe,
And does not need our sympathies. The rain
But fits the shorn field for new yield of grain;
    While the red, brazen skies, the sun's fierce glow,
    The dry, hot winds that from the tropics blow
Do parch and wither the unsheltered plain.
The anguish that through long, remorseless years
    Looks out upon the world with no relief
Of sudden tempests or slow-dripping tears—
    The still, unuttered, silent, wordless grief
That evermore doth ache, and ache, and ache—
This is the sorrow wherewith hearts do break.

THE CREED.

Whoever was begotten by pure love,
And came desired and welcome into life,
Is of immaculate conception. He
Whose heart is full of tenderness and truth,
Who loves mankind more than he loves himself,
And cannot find room in his heart for hate,
May be another Christ. We all may be
The Saviours of the world if we believe
In the Divinity which dwells in us
And worship it, and nail our grosser selves,
Our tempers, greeds, and our unworthy aims,
Upon the cross. Who giveth love to all;
Pays kindness for unkindness, smiles for frowns;
And lends new courage to each fainting heart,
And strengthens hope and scatters joy abroad—
He, too, is a Redeemer, Son of God.

"CAME DESIRED AND WELCOMED INTO LIFE"

PROGRESS.

Let there be many windows to your soul,
That all the glory of the universe
May beautify it. Not the narrow pane
Of one poor creed can catch the radiant rays
That shine from countless sources. Tear away
The blinds of superstition; let the light
Pour through fair windows broad as Truth itself
And high as God.

                Why should the spirit peer
Through some priest-curtained orifice, and grope
Along dim corridors of doubt, when all
The splendor from unfathomed seas of space
Might bathe it with the golden waves of Love?
Sweep up the debris of decaying faiths;
Sweep down the cobwebs of worn-out beliefs,
And throw your soul wide open to the light
Of Reason and of Knowledge. Tune your ear
To all the wordless music of the stars
And to the voice of Nature, and your heart
Shall turn to truth and goodness as the plant
Turns to the sun. A thousand unseen hands
Reach down to help you to their peace-crowned heights.
And all the forces of the firmament
Shall fortify your strength. Be not afraid
To thrust aside half-truths and grasp the whole.

MY FRIEND.

When first I looked upon the face of Pain
    I shrank repelled, as one shrinks from a foe
    Who stands with dagger poised, as for a blow.
I was in search of Pleasure and of Gain;
I turned aside to let him pass: in vain;
    He looked straight in my eyes and would not go.
    "Shake hands," he said; "our paths are one, and so
We must be comrades on the way, 'tis plain."

I felt the firm clasp of his hand on mine;
    Through all my veins it sent a strengthening glow.
    I straightway linked my arm in his, and lo!
He led me forth to joys almost divine;
    With God's great truths enriched me in the end:
    And now I hold him as my dearest friend.

CREATION.

The impulse of all love is to create.
    God was so full of love, in his embrace
    He clasped the empty nothingness of space,
And low! the solar system! High in state
The mighty sun sat, so supreme and great
    With this same essence, one smile of its face
    Brought myriad forms of life forth; race on race,
From insects up to men.

                Through love, not hate,
All that is grand in nature or in art
    Sprang into being. He who would build sublime
    And lasting works, to stand the test of time,
Must inspiration draw from his full heart.
    And he who loveth widely, well, and much,
    The secret holds of the true master touch.

RED CARNATIONS.

One time in Arcadie's fair bowers
    There met a bright immortal band,
To choose their emblems from the flowers
    That made an Eden of that land.

Sweet Constancy, with eyes of hope,
    Strayed down the garden path alone
And gathered sprays of heliotrope,
    To place in clusters at her zone.

True Friendship plucked the ivy green,
    Forever fresh, forever fair.
Inconstancy with flippant mien
    The fading primrose chose to wear.

One moment Love the rose paused by;
    But Beauty picked it for her hair.
Love paced the garden with a sigh
    He found no fitting emblem there.

Then suddenly he saw a flame,
    A conflagration turned to bloom;
It even put the rose to shame,
    Both in its beauty and perfume.

He watched it, and it did not fade;
    He plucked it, and it brighter grew.
In cold or heat, all undismayed,
    It kept its fragrance and its hue.

"Here deathless love and passion sleep,"
    He cried, "embodied in this flower.
This is the emblem I will keep."
    Love wore carnations from that hour.

LIFE IS TOO SHORT.

Life is too short for any vain regretting;
    Let dead delight bury its dead, I say,
And let us go upon our way forgetting
    The joys and sorrows of each yesterday
Between the swift sun's rising and its setting
We have no time for useless tears or fretting:
                    Life is too short.

Life is too short for any bitter feeling;
    Time is the best avenger if we wait;
The years speed by, and on their wings bear healing;
    We have no room for anything like hate.
This solemn truth the low mounds seem revealing
That thick and fast about our feet are stealing:
                    Life is too short.

Life is too short for aught but high endeavor—
    Too short for spite, but long enough for love.
And love lives on forever and forever;
    It links the worlds that circle on above:
'Tis God's first law, the universe's lever.
In His vast realm the radiant souls sigh never
                    "Life is too short."

A SCULPTOR.

As the ambitious sculptor, tireless, lifts
    Chisel and hammer to the block at hand,
    Before my half-formed character I stand
And ply the shining tools of mental gifts.
    I'll cut away a huge, unsightly side
Of selfishness, and smooth to curves of grace
The angles of ill-temper.

              And no trace
    Shall my sure hammer leave of silly pride.
Chip after chip must fall from vain desires,
    And the sharp corners of my discontent
    Be rounded into symmetry, and lent
Great harmony by faith that never tires.
    Unfinished still, I must toil on and on,
    Till the pale critic, Death, shall say, "'Tis done."

BEYOND.

It seemeth such a little way to me
    Across to that strange country—the Beyond;
And yet, not strange, for it has grown to be
    The home of those of whom I am so fond,
They make it seem familiar and most dear,
As journeying friends bring distant regions near.

So close it lies that when my sight is clear
    I think I almost see the gleaming strand.
I know I feel those who have gone from here
    Come near enough sometimes to touch my hand.
I often think, but for our veiled eyes,
We should find Heaven right round about us lies.

I cannot make it seem a day to dread,
    When from this dear earth I shall journey out
To that still dearer country of the dead,
    And join the lost ones, so long dreamed about.
I love this world, yet shall I love to go
And meet the friends who wait for me, I know.

I never stand above a bier and see
    The seal of death set on some well-loved face
But that I think, "One more to welcome me
    When I shall cross the intervening space

Between this land and that one 'over there';
One more to make the strange Beyond seem fair."

And so for me there is no sting to death,
　　And so the grave has lost its victory.
It is but crossing—with a bated breath
　　And white, set face—a little strip of sea
To find the loved ones waiting on the shore,
More beautiful, more precious than before.

THE SADDEST HOUR.

The saddest hour of anguish and of loss
    Is not that season of supreme despair
    When we can find no least light anywhere
To gild the dread, black shadow of the Cross;
Not in that luxury of sorrow when
    We sup on salt of tears, and drink the gall
    Of memories of days beyond recall—
Of lost delights that cannot come again.

    But when, with eyes that are no longer wet,
We look out on the great, wide world of men,
And, smiling, lean toward a bright tomorrow,
    Then backward shrink, with sudden keen regret,
    To find that we are learning to forget:
Ah! then we face the saddest hour of sorrow.

ACROSS THE SEA OF SILENCE

SHOW ME THE WAY.

Show me the way that leads to the true life.
    I do not care what tempests may assail me,
I shall be given courage for the strife;
    I know my strength will not desert or fail me;
I know that I shall conquer in the fray:
                Show me the way.

Show me the way up to a higher plane,
    Where body shall be servant to the soul.
I do not care what tides of woe or pain
    Across my life their angry waves may roll,
If I but reach the end I seek, some day:
                Show me the way.

Show me the way, and let me bravely climb
    Above vain grievings for unworthy treasures;
Above all sorrow that finds balm in time;
    Above small triumphs or belittling pleasures;
Up to those heights where these things seem child's-play:
                Show me the way.

Show me the way to that calm, perfect peace
    Which springs from an inward consciousness of right;
To where all conflicts with the flesh shall cease,
    And self shall radiate with the spirit's light.
Though hard the journey and the strife, I pray,
                    Show me the way.

MY HERITAGE.

I into life so full of love was sent
    That all the shadows which fall on the way
    Of every human being could not stay,
But fled before the light my spirit lent.

I saw the world through gold and crimson dyes:
    Men sighed and said, "Those rosy hues will fade
    As you pass on into the glare and shade!"
Still beautiful the way seems to mine eyes.

They said, "You are too jubilant and glad;
    The world is full of sorrow and of wrong.
    Full soon your lips shall breathe forth sighs—not song."
The day wears on, and yet I am not sad.

They said, "You love too largely, and you must,
    Through wound on wound, grow bitter to your kind."
    They were false prophets; day by day I find
More cause for love, and less cause for distrust.

They said, "Too free you give your soul's rare wine;
    The world will quaff, but it will not repay."
    Yet in the emptied flagons, day by day,
True hearts pour back a nectar as divine.

Thy heritage! Is it not love's estate?
    Look to it, then, and keep its soil well tilled.
    I hold that my best wishes are fulfilled
Because I love so much, and cannot hate.

RESOLVE.

Build on resolve, and not upon regret,
    The structure of thy future. Do not grope
Among the shadows of old sins, but let
    Thine own soul's light shine on the path of hope
And dissipate the darkness. Waste no tears
Upon the blotted record of lost years,
But turn the leaf and smile, oh, smile, to see
The fair white pages that remain for thee.

Prate not of thy repentance. But believe
    The spark divine dwells in thee: let it grow.
That which the upreaching spirit can achieve
    The grand and all-creative forces know;
They will assist and strengthen as the light
Lifts up the acorn to the oak tree's height.
Thou hast but to resolve, and lo! God's whole
Great universe shall fortify thy soul.

AT ELEUSIS.

I, at Eleusis, saw the finest sight,
    When early morning's banners were unfurled.
    From high Olympus, gazing on the world,
The ancient gods once saw it with delight.
Sad Demeter had in a single night
    Removed her sombre garments! and mine eyes
    Beheld a 'broidered mantle in pale dyes
Thrown o'er her throbbing bosom. Sweet and clear
There fell the sound of music on mine ear.
    And from the South came Hermes, he whose lyre
    One time appeased the great Apollo's ire.
The rescued maid, Persephone, by the hand
He led to waiting Demeter, and cheer
And light and beauty once more blessed the land.

COURAGE.

There is a courage, a majestic thing
  That springs forth from the brow of pain, full-grown,
  Minerva-like, and dares all dangers known,
And all the threatening future yet may bring;
Crowned with the helmet of great suffering;
  Serene with that grand strength by martyrs shown,
  When at the stake they die and make no moan,
And even as the flames leap up are heard to sing:

A courage so sublime and unafraid,
  It wears its sorrows like a coat of mail;
  And Fate, the archer, passes by dismayed,
Knowing his best barbed arrows needs must fail
To pierce a soul so armored and arrayed
  That Death himself might look on it and quail.

SOLITUDE.

Laugh, and the world laughs with you;
    Weep, and you weep alone;
For the sad old earth must borrow its mirth,
    But has trouble enough of its own.
Sing, and the hills will answer;
    Sigh, it is lost on the air;
The echoes bound to a joyful sound,
    But shrink from voicing care.

Rejoice, and men will seek you;
    Grieve, and they turn and go;
They want full measure of all your pleasure,
    But they do not need your woe.
Be glad, and your friends are many;
    Be sad, and you lose them all;
There are none to decline your nectar'd wine,
    But alone you must drink life's gall.

Feast, and your halls are crowded;
    Fast, and the world goes by.
Succeed and give, and it helps you live,
    But no man can help you die.
There is room in the halls of pleasure
    For a large and lordly train,
But one by one we must all file on
    Through the narrow aisles of pain.

THE YEAR OUTGROWS THE SPRING.

The year outgrows the spring it thought so sweet,
    And clasps the summer with a new delight,
Yet wearied, leaves her languors and her heat
    When cool-browed autumn dawns upon his sight.

The tree outgrows the bud's suggestive grace,
    And feels new pride in blossoms fully blown.
But even this to deeper joy gives place
    When bending boughs 'neath blushing burdens groan.

Life's rarest moments are derived from change.
    The heart outgrows old happiness, old grief,
And suns itself in feelings new and strange;
    The most enduring pleasure is but brief.

Our tastes, our needs, are never twice the same.
    Nothing contents us long, however dear.
The spirit in us, like the grosser frame,
    Outgrows the garments which it wore last year.

Change is the watchword of Progression. When
    We tire of well-worn ways we seek for new.
This restless craving in the souls of men
    Spurs them to climb, and seek the mountain view.

So let who will erect an altar shrine
     To meek-browed Constancy, and sing her praise.
Unto enlivening Change I shall build mine,
     Who lends new zest and interest to my days.

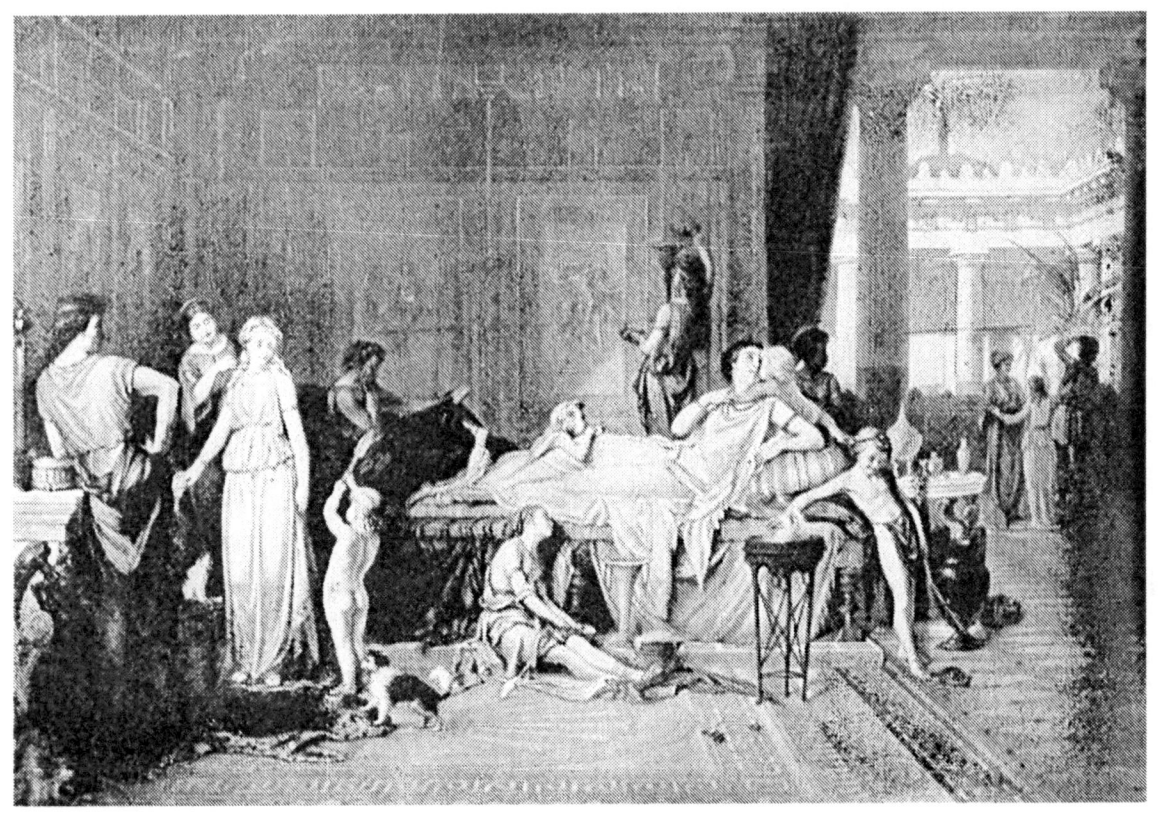

"...AND LIGHT AND BEAUTY BLESSED
THE LAND"

THE BEAUTIFUL LAND OF NOD.

Come, cuddle your head on my shoulder, dear,
    Your head like the golden-rod,
And we will go sailing away from here
    To the beautiful Land of Nod.
Away from life's hurry and flurry and worry,
    Away from earth's shadows and gloom,
To a world of fair weather we'll float off together,
    Where roses are always in bloom.

Just shut your eyes and fold your hands,
    Your hands like the leaves of a rose,
And we will go sailing to those fair lands
    That never an atlas shows.
On the North and the West they are bounded by rest,
    On the South and the East, by dreams;
'Tis the country ideal, where nothing is real,
    But everything only seems.

Just drop down the curtains of your dear eyes
    Those eyes like a bright bluebell,
And we will sail out under starlit skies,
    To the land where the fairies dwell.

Down the river of sleep our barque shall sweep,
Till it reaches that mystical Isle
Which no man hath seen, but where all have been,
And there we will pause awhile.
I will croon you a song as we float along
To that shore that is blessed of God,
Then, ho! for that fair land, we're off for that rare land,
That beautiful Land of Nod.

THE TIGER.

In the still jungle of the senses lay
A tiger soundly sleeping, till one day
A bold young hunter chanced to come that way.

"How calm," he said, "that splendid creature lies!
I long to rouse him into swift surprise."
The well aimed arrow shot from amorous eyes,

And lo! the tiger rouses up and turns,
A coal of fire his glowing eyeball burns,
His mighty frame with savage hunger yearns.

He crouches for a spring; his eyes dilate—
Alas! bold hunter, what shall be thy fate?
Thou canst not fly; it is too late, too late.

Once having tasted human flesh, ah! then,
Woe, woe unto the whole rash world of men.
The wakened tiger will not sleep again.

ONLY A SIMPLE RHYME.

Only a simple rhyme of love and sorrow,
    Where "blisses" rhymed with "kisses," "heart," with "dart:"
Yet, reading it, new strength I seemed to borrow,
    To live on bravely and to do my part.

A little rhyme about a heart that's bleeding—
    Of lonely hours and sorrow's unrelief:
I smiled at first; but there came with the reading
    A sense of sweet companionship in grief.

The selfishness of my own woe forsaking,
    I thought about the singer of that song.
Some other breast felt this same weary aching;
    Another found the summer days too long.

The few sad lines, my sorrow so expressing,
    I read, and on the singer, all unknown,
I breathed a fervent though a silent blessing,
    And seemed to clasp his hand within my own.

And though fame pass him and he never know it,
    And though he never sings another strain,
He has performed the mission of the poet,
    In helping some sad heart to bear its pain.

314

I WILL BE WORTHY OF IT.

I may not reach the heights I seek,
    My untried strength may fail me,
Or, half-way up the mountain peak,
    Fierce tempests may assail me.
But though that place I never gain,
Herein lies comfort for my pain—
                I will be worthy of it.

I may not triumph in success,
    Despite my earnest labor;
I may not grasp results that bless
    The efforts of my neighbor;
But though my goal I never see,
This thought shall always dwell with me—
                I will be worthy of it.

The golden glory of Love's light
    May never fall on my way;
My path may always lead through night,
    Like some deserted by-way;
But though life's dearest joy I miss
There lies a nameless strength in this—
                I will be worthy of it.

SONNET.

Methinks ofttimes my heart is like some bee
    That goes forth through the summer day and sings.
    And gathers honey from all growing things
In garden plot or on the clover lea.

When the long afternoon grows late, and she
    Would seek her hive, she cannot lift her wings.
    So heavily the too sweet bin den clings,
From which she would not, and yet would, fly free.

So with my full, fond heart; for when it tries
    To lift itself to peace crowned heights, above
    The common way where countless feet have trod,
Lo! then, this burden of dear human ties,
    This growing weight of precious earthly love,
    Binds down the spirit that would soar to God.

REGRET.

There is a haunting phantom called Regret,
    A shadowy creature robed somewhat like Woe,
    But fairer in the face, whom all men know
By her sad mien and eyes forever wet.
No heart would seek her; but once having met,
    All take her by the hand, and to and fro
    They wander through those paths of long ago—
Those hallowed ways 'twere wiser to forget.

One day she led me to that lost land's gate
    And bade me enter; but I answered "No!
I will pass on with my bold comrade, Fate;
    I have no tears to waste on thee—no time;
    My strength I hoard for heights I hope to climb:
No friend art thou for souls that would be great."

"... THE STRIFE THAT IS WEARYING ME"

LET ME LEAN HARD.

Let me lean hard upon the Eternal Breast:
In all earth's devious ways I sought for rest
And found it not. I will be strong, said I,
And lean upon myself. I will not cry
And importune all heaven with my complaint.
But now my strength fails, and I fall, I faint:
Let me lean hard.

Let me lean hard upon the unfailing Arm.
I said I will walk on, I fear no harm,
The spark divine within my soul will show
The upward pathway where my feet should go.
But now the heights to which I most aspire
Are lost in clouds. I stumble and I tire:
Let me lean hard.

Let me lean harder yet. That swerveless force
Which speeds the solar systems on their course
Can take, unfelt, the burden of my woe,
Which bears me to the dust and hurts me so.
I thought my strength enough for any fate,
But lo! I sink beneath my sorrow's weight:
Let me lean hard.

PENALTY.

Because of the fullness of what I had
    All that I have seems void and vain.
If I had not been happy I were not sad;
    Though my salt is savorless, why complain?

From the ripe perfection of what was mine,
    All that is mine seems worse than naught;
Yet I know as I sit in the dark and pine,
    No cup could be drained which had not been fraught.

From the throb and thrill of a day that was,
    The day that now is seems dull with gloom;
Yet I bear its dullness and darkness because
    'Tis but the reaction of glow and bloom.

From the royal feast which of old was spread
    I am starved on the diet which now is mine;
Yet I could not turn hungry from water and bread,
    If I had not been sated on fruit and wine.

SUNSET.

I saw the day lean o'er the world's sharp edge
    And peer into night's chasm, dark and damp;
    High in his hand he held a blazing lamp,
Then dropped it and plunged headlong down the ledge.

With lurid splendor that swift paled to gray,
    I saw the dim skies suddenly flush bright.
    'Twas but the expiring glory of the light
Flung from the hand of the adventurous day.

THE WHEEL OF THE BREAST.

Through rivers of veins on the nameless quest
    The tide of my life goes hurriedly sweeping,
Till it reaches that curious wheel o' the breast,
The human heart, which is never at rest.
    Faster, faster, it cries, and leaping,
Plunging, dashing, speeding away,
The wheel and the river work night and day.

I know not wherefore, I know not whither,
    This strange tide rushes with such mad force:
It glides on hither, it slides on thither,
    Over and over the selfsame course,
    With never an outlet and never a source;
And it lashes itself to the heat of passion
And whirls the heart in a mill-wheel fashion.

I can hear in the hush of the still, still night,
    The ceaseless sound of that mighty river;
I can hear it gushing, gurgling, rushing,
With a wild, delirious, strange delight,
And a conscious pride in its sense of might,
    As it hurries and worries my heart forever.

And I wonder oft as I lie awake,
    And list to the river that seethes and surges
Over the wheel that it chides and urges—
I wonder oft if that wheel will break
    With the mighty pressure it bears, some day,
    Or slowly and wearily wear away.

For little by little the heart is wearing,
Like the wheel of the mill, as the tide goes tearing
    And plunging hurriedly through my breast,
    In a network of veins on a nameless quest,
From and forth, unto unknown oceans,
Bringing its cargoes of fierce emotions,
    With never a pause or an hour for rest.

A MEETING.

Quite carelessly I turned the newsy sheet;
　　A song I sang, full many a year ago,
Smiled up at me, as in a busy street
　　One meets an old-time friend he used to know.

So full it was, that simple little song,
　　Of all the hope, the transport, and the truth,
Which to the impetuous morn of life belong,
　　That once again I seemed to grasp my youth.

So full it was of that sweet, fancied pain
　　We woo and cherish ere we meet with woe,
I felt as one who hears a plaintive strain
　　His mother sang him in the long ago.

Up from the grave the years that lay between
　　That song's birthday and my stern present came
Like phantom forms and swept across the scene,
　　Bearing their broken dreams of love and fame.

Fair hopes and bright ambitions that I knew
　　In that old time, with their ideal grace,
Shone for a moment, then were lost to view
　　Behind the dull clouds of the commonplace.

With trembling hands I put the sheet away;
    Ah, little song! the sad and bitter truth
Struck like an arrow when we met that day!
    My life has missed the promise of its youth.

EARNESTNESS.

The hurry of the times affects us so
    In this swift rushing hour, we crowd and press
And thrust each other backward as we go,
    And do not pause to lay sufficient stress
    Upon that good, strong, true word, Earnestness.
In our impetuous haste, could we but know
Its full, deep meaning, its vast import, oh,
    Then might we grasp the secret of success!
In that receding age when men were great,
    The bone and sinew of their purpose lay
    In this one word. God likes an earnest soul—
Too earnest to be eager. Soon or late
    It leaves the spent horde breathless by the way,
    And stands serene, triumphant at the goal.

A PICTURE.

I strolled last eve across the lonely down;
    One solitary picture struck my eye:
    A distant ploughboy stood against the sky—
How far he seemed above the noisy town!

Upon the bosom of a cloud the sod
    Laid its bruised cheek as he moved slowly by,
    And, watching him, I asked myself if I
In very truth stood half as near to God.

TWIN-BORN.

He who possesses virtue at its best,
 Or greatness in the true sense of the word,
 Has one day started even with that herd
Whose swift feet now speed but at sin's behest.
It is the same force in the human breast
 Which makes men gods or demons. If we gird
 Those strong emotions by which we are stirred
With might of will and purpose, heights unguessed
 Shall dawn for us; or if we give them sway
We can sink down and consort with the lost.
All virtue is worth just the price it cost.
 Black sin is oft white truth that missed its way
And wandered off in paths not understood.
Twin-born I hold great evil and great good.

FLOODS.

In the dark night, from sweet refreshing sleep
    I wake to hear outside my window-pane
    The uncurbed fury of the wild spring rain,
And weird winds lashing the defiant deep,
And roar of floods that gather strength and leap
    Down dizzy, wreck-strewn channels to the main.
    I turn upon my pillow and again
Compose myself for slumber.
                    Let them sweep;
    I once survived great floods, and do not fear,
Though ominous planets congregate, and seem
To foretell strange disasters.
                    From a dream—
    Ah! dear God! such a dream!—I woke to hear,
Through the dense shadows lit by no star's gleam,
    The rush of mighty waters on my ear.
Helpless, afraid, and all alone, I lay;
    The floods had come upon me unaware.
    I heard the crash of structures that were fair;
The bridges of fond hopes were swept away
By great salt waves of sorrow. In dismay
    I saw by the red lightning's lurid glare
    That on the rock-bound island of despair
I had been cast. Till the dim dawn of day
    I heard my castles falling, and the roll

Of angry billows bearing to the sea
    The broken timbers of my very soul.
    Were all the pent-up waters from the whole
Stupendous solar system to break free,
There are no floods that now can frighten me.

A FABLE.

Some cawing Crows, a hooting Owl,
A Hawk, a Canary, an old Marsh-Fowl,
    One day all meet together
To hold a caucus and settle the fate
Of a certain bird (without a mate),
    A bird of another feather.

"My friends," said the Owl, with a look most wise,
"The Eagle is soaring too near the skies,
    In a way that is quite improper;
Yet the world is praising her, so I'm told,
And I think her actions have grown so bold
    That some of us ought to stop her."

"I have heard it said," quoth Hawk, with a sigh,
"That young lambs died at the glance of her eye,
    And I wholly scorn and despise her.
This, and more, I am told they say,
And I think that the only proper way
    Is never to recognize her."

"I am quite convinced," said Crow, with a caw,
"That the Eagle minds no moral law,
　　She's a most unruly creature."
"She's an ugly thing," piped Canary Bird;
"Some call her handsome—it's so absurd—
　　She hasn't a decent feature."

Then the old Marsh-Hen went hopping about,
She said she was sure—*she* hadn't a doubt—
　　Of the truth of each bird's story:
And she thought it a duty to stop her flight,
To pull her down from her lofty height,
　　And take the gilt from her glory.

But, lo! from a peak on the mountain grand
That looks out over the smiling land
　　And over the mighty ocean,
The Eagle is spreading her splendid wings—
She rises, rises, and upward swings,
　　With a slow, majestic motion.

Up in the blue of God's own skies,
With a cry of rapture, away she flies,
　　Close to the Great Eternal:
She sweeps the world with her piercing sight;
Her soul is filled with the infinite
　　And the joy of things supernal.

Thus rise forever the chosen of God,
The genius-crowned or the power-shod,
    Over the dust-world sailing;
And back, like splinters blown by the winds,
Must fall the missiles of silly minds,
    Useless and unavailing.

BIBLIOBAZAAR

The essential book market!

Did you know that you can get any of our titles in large print?

Did you know that we have an ever-growing collection of books in many languages?

Order online:
www.bibliobazaar.com

Find all of your favorite classic books!

Stay up to date with the latest government reports!

At BiblioBazaar, we aim to make knowledge more accessible by making thousands of titles available to you- *quickly and affordably.*

Contact us:
BiblioBazaar
PO Box 21206
Charleston, SC 29413

Lightning Source UK Ltd.
Milton Keynes UK
22 April 2010

153215UK00004B/19/A